Oh, Christmas Night

Oh, Christmas Night

Jane Porter

TULE
PUBLISHING

Oh, Christmas Night
Copyright © 2019 Jane Porter
Tule Publishing First Printing, November 2019

The Tule Publishing, Inc.

ALL RIGHTS RESERVED

First Publication by Tule Publishing 2019

No part of this book may be used or reproduced in any manner whatsoever without written permission except in the case of brief quotations embodied in critical articles and reviews.

This is a work of fiction. Names, characters, places, and incidents are products of the author's imagination or are used fictitiously. Any resemblance to actual events, locales, organizations, or persons, living or dead, is entirely coincidental.

ISBN: 978-1-951190-78-1

Dedication

For Maggie Marr
who encourages my dreams!

Acknowledgements

Thank you to Alissa Callen for sharing her bookstore, Paradise Books, and her lovely characters Lesley and Nash with me. I am grateful for your generosity and how Marietta magic lives on!

Thank you to the magnificent Kelly Hunter for editing **Oh, Christmas Night**. Your suggestions were spot on and helped shape Atticus and Rachel's story, giving them the happy-ever-after they deserved.

Thank you for to the Tule team for having my back, especially Cyndi and Meghan for brainstorming and Jenny for being an early reader. Couldn't have gotten through this one without you!

Thank you Ty Gurney and my boys for being patient while I rewrote chapter 1 twenty times, and then chapter 2 about twenty five times….and so on, and so on.

Thank you to my favorite librarian in the world, John Charles. John, I'm lucky to call you my friend, and grateful you always look out for me.

Thank you to my readers who encourage me and keep me wanting to tell new stories. You are truly the best.

And lastly, thank you to Brenda Novak, who is something of my very own guardian angel. So much love to you for all your support over the years.

xo

Chapter One

Rachel Mills felt positively ill. She sat down at her desk, and covered her face with her hands, struggling to breathe.

She didn't get the promotion.

She'd been passed over, *again*.

Her throat thickened and her eyes burned, hot and gritty. It didn't make sense. No one in her department had more experience, or a better work ethic, than she did. No one at Novak & Bartley put in more hours, or handled more, clients than she did.

How could they promote Jay Shields over her? He'd been hired three years after her. He used up every bit of his vacation time each year, every year, and then some. He frequently made mistakes requiring her to go in and clean up after him. She routinely solved problems he couldn't. So why reward *him*?

Rachel didn't want to believe it was because Jay was a man. She really, truly didn't want to go there… but every person promoted these past few years had been a man. Plenty of women worked at Novak & Bartley, but most in support positions. She'd known this going in, too, but she'd viewed the lack of female leadership as an opportunity to prove herself.

And she had.

She'd gone over and above, time and again. She'd brought in new clients, increased the firm's revenue, and had saved important accounts that were unhappy and wanted to go.

She'd done the research and crunched the numbers, and knew what was required to be promoted, too. She understood that one couldn't ask for, or expect, more responsibility if one wasn't adding sufficient value, which was why she was handling big accounts, and big money, and she didn't make mistakes.

So why was she not recognized?

Rachel squeezed her eyes closed, air bottling in her lungs. She was hurt, but even more so, she was angry. The first oversight had been disappointing, but to be passed over three times? To be given flimsy excuses by upper management?

She wasn't a child. She didn't appreciate being patronized. But, really, she had no one else to blame. She'd known during the interview process eight years ago that she'd be one of the only female accountants at the firm, but it hadn't worried her. She'd naively thought she'd be able to prove to them they'd hired the right person, and she'd demonstrate competency and excellence and she'd be the first of many women to work for Novak & Bartley.

But that hadn't been the case.

Yes, a few female accountants had been hired after her, but none of them had been given a chance for advancement. None of them were invited to participate in Novak & Bartley's annual golf tournament or the other VIP client events, either. It was as if they'd all hit a glass ceiling—and in this case, the ceiling was very, very low.

A light knock sounded on her door and Rachel lifted her head to see Alicia, one of the young women that worked in administration, standing in the doorway with a bright yellow package.

"I knew you'd be here," Alicia said confidently. "Lots of the others have already left for Thanksgiving."

"Thanksgiving isn't for another two days," Rachel answered, sitting taller, squaring her shoulders. "What are your plans for the holiday? Going anywhere?"

"Heading to Santa Barbara. My boyfriend's family is there."

"Nice."

"What about you?"

Rachel gestured to the boxes stacked in the corner. "Probably here, preparing for the SynTan audit."

"That's not for months."

"Early January, but it's better to be prepared."

"You're the queen of prepared," Alicia said, smiling as she handed the package over. "This just arrived. It's from Australia. Do we have clients in Australia?"

"I don't," Rachel answered, straightening. "Not sure about the firm."

Alicia disappeared and Rachel turned the thick, padded DHL envelope over to read the address label. It had been sent from Lesley Hart, Rachel's godmother, a godmother Rachel had only met a couple of times in her life, the last time being at Rachel's mother's funeral twelve years ago. Rachel had been a senior in high school and the funeral had been a blur of tears and hugs, as well as her father's stoic silence, and after it was all over, she just wanted to put it behind her. She wanted to forget the pain and grief and she buried herself in her studies, because the one thing in life that didn't let her down was numbers. Numbers never failed, and numbers never lied. Little wonder she chose accounting as her college major.

Uncertain as to what this mythical godmother had sent her, Rachel opened the envelope and drew out another envelope, this one bumpy with a letter, a folder of papers, and a key on a small key ring with a painted decorative accent that read "Big Sky."

Frowning, Rachel held the key ring for a moment, the key pressed to her palm. Years ago her mother talked about being from Big Sky country, but Rachel had only been there once, and she was so young at the time that she didn't remember it. Setting the key aside, she read the brief letter, and then read it again, more baffled with every reading.

It seemed that her godmother, the one she'd only met a

handful of times, was gifting her a bookstore. In Montana. In the town where Rachel's mother had grown up.

Perplexed, she read the letter a third time.

My dear Rachel,

I apologize for missing your 30th birthday last month, but hope it was happy. I thought of you on your special day, and I thought of your mother, too, and how proud she'd be of you. I'm sorry I haven't been a better godmother but please know I carry you and your mother in my heart.

To celebrate your 30th birthday, and your impressive accomplishments, I am giving you Paradise Books, my bookstore in Marietta. I can't imagine anyone more deserving. May it bring you the joy it brought me.

With all my love,
Lesley

Rachel blinked hard, the sudden rise of emotion catching her off guard, not just by the gift, but by the mention of her mother. No one mentioned her mother anymore. Dad certainly didn't discuss her, and Rachel didn't think of her, either, finding the memories too painful.

Rachel folded the letter, hiding the words and the emotion, and reached for the paperwork. There was a great deal of paperwork, too, as the gifting of a business, even a small business, wasn't a small thing. The government didn't just let one "gift" a business. There were taxes and paperwork, and more taxes, things Rachel knew well as a corporate tax specialist.

The paperwork included a description of the business—a historic red brick building which included an apartment carved from the attic rafters, allowing the owner to both live and work on the historic premises—along with the most recent tax returns on the building which indicated that the store hadn't been open in several years.

Lesley shared in a handwritten note that the turn of the century brick building was paid for, and the property taxes had been taken care of for the next year, but she was aware that Rachel would incur some taxes with the gift and she hoped that the taxes wouldn't be an undue burden. There was value in the store, but to be honest, most of the value was in the building itself, and Lesley suggested Rachel visit Marietta and see the store for herself. In fact, Lesley added, if she had time, she should go soon since Christmas was one of the nicest times of years in Marietta.

Exasperated, Rachel pushed the paperwork away, and turned in her chair to glance out the office window with its view of the 405 freeway and the tall Ferris wheel at Irvine Spectrum.

What was she supposed to do with a bookstore in Montana? Rachel's entire world was here. She'd been born and raised in Irvine, attending UC Irvine where she'd studied accounting, and Irvine was where she lived now, just seven miles from Novak & Bartley's main office. How did one just pop into Marietta for a visit? It wasn't close. It wasn't convenient. And this wasn't a gift Rachel could use.

Weren't fairy godmothers supposed to show up when you needed them? Weren't they supposed to swoop in and make things better?

Rachel turned from the window, her gaze sweeping in her office with the towering pile of files, and boxes of documents stacked in the corners, and it struck her quite forcefully that she'd sacrificed almost everything for this company and suddenly she wasn't sure the sacrifices had been worth it. She'd let go of relationships and friendships for longer work hours, and how had it mattered? She wasn't getting anywhere. And even if she stayed with Novak & Bartley, it was unlikely she'd ever make partner.

Exhaling hard, she reached for the keychain with the Big Sky accent, and turned it over, the worn brass smooth against her skin. She couldn't remember when she'd felt so devastated.

She'd poured herself into her job. She'd sacrificed virtually everything for work. There had been a plan, and it had looked so neat and tidy on paper. X number of clients times Y number of years and she'd be a manager, and then a director, and eventually a partner. Only it wasn't working out that way. Her numbers were letting her down—no, Rachel stopped herself, that wasn't true. It wasn't the numbers that let her down. It was people.

So, what was she going to do? Go somewhere else, do

something else, or just put her head down and work harder? Rachel didn't know. She couldn't think. She couldn't get perspective.

She craved air, and space, and a chance to relax. Breathe.

Maybe a visit to this old bookstore in the middle of nowhere was exactly what she needed.

ATTICUS EVAN BOWEN, much like his namesake Atticus Finch, was an attorney from the South, unlike the fictional Finch, Atticus Bowen was from Houston, Texas, not Maycomb, Alabama, and his specialty was real estate law.

Atticus loved making deals, and nothing was more rewarding than closing a very challenging deal. After a stint as a litigation attorney, he'd switched to real estate law and had found his niche because he wasn't afraid of hard conversations and tough negotiations. Where others might shrink from conflict, he felt encouraged, even empowered. Through experience he'd learned to rely on reason, not emotion, and so far, reason had never let him down.

His mother—who'd named him Atticus because *To Kill a Mockingbird* was her favorite novel—had said that her Atticus was pragmatic from the start, refusing to put in an appearance for nine days after his due date, choosing to stay put until the torrential rains flooding Houston had ended, and the streets had dried. No, Atticus Bowen was nothing but practical, and he exhausted his parents and teachers with his logic, as well as his ability to withstand stress and uncomfortable situations, virtually guaranteeing that, in the end, he got what he wanted. As a boy, it was winning chess tournaments and baseball games. As an adult, he acquired buildings, businesses, opportunities.

There was an opportunity before him now, and he was determined to seize it.

"Lesley, you know I want that building," he said calmly, shifting the cell phone to his other ear. "We've been doing this for over a year. Tell me what you want. I want to make this happen, and I'll be more than fair."

"Atticus, it's out of my hands now—"

"Do you want me to fly to Australia? Would you feel better if you met me in person? I'll get on the next flight, if that's the issue."

"Of course I'd love to meet you, Atticus, but that's not the issue. You see, I don't own Paradise Books anymore. I've given the bookstore to my goddaughter. Rachel is the owner now. It's up to Rachel to decide what she'd like to do with the place."

Atticus had to hold his breath and count to five. "When did this happen?" he asked when he was certain he could speak calmly.

"Rather recently. It was a belated birthday gift." Her tone turned apologetic. "I'm sorry to disappoint you, but I just wasn't ready to see my beloved bookstore become a barbecue joint."

"Galveston doesn't serve barbecue. It's a steak house. An upscale steak house."

"But it still meant the books would go, wouldn't it? And that would be such a shame."

He counted to five again. "Your goddaughter, Rachel. She lives in Marietta?"

"No. She's from Southern California. She's an accountant and very clever, very successful. I'm terribly proud of her."

Atticus was glad the older woman couldn't see him roll his eyes. "What is Rachel going to do with a bookstore if she lives in California?"

"I don't know. That's up to her."

"I'd like to reach out to her."

"I'm sure you would," Lesley said primly.

He smashed his sigh of exasperation. "Would you mind sharing her contact details with me?"

"Actually, I'm not sure I should, not without her permission. However, I understand she'll be spending the next week in Marietta, so you might be able to catch her at Paradise Books." She hesitated before adding lightly, "If you are willing to jump on a plane."

So, to Montana he went, even though it was Thanksgiving weekend.

He flew in Saturday night, checked in to the Graff Hotel, and then walked the three blocks to have a look at Paradise Books on Main Street.

The wind gusted and howled as he stood on the corner, looking up at the two-story, corner building he'd admired ever since he first visited the charming Paradise Valley town two and a half years ago. This building would be the perfect location for his first Galveston Steak House in Montana.

Atticus had started Galveston ten years ago with friends. He hadn't put a lot of money into the first restaurant, but he'd handled all the paperwork and contracts, and proved his value when the new restaurant was hit with its first lawsuit filed by a disgruntled former chef. Atticus handled the lawsuit quickly and quietly and, before long, one location became two, and then four, and then seven. But as the Galveston brand grew, so did the problems, and maybe they were just little things to other people, but little things added up to big things, and when a huge financial setback threatened to close the seven restaurants dotting Texas, Nevada, California and Colorado, he stepped in, bought his partners out, and became the sole owner.

He liked being the sole owner, too, and as sole owner he'd made changes to the restaurants, improving the menu, improving the service, and bumping up prices, because when people went to a good steak house, they expected great steaks and expensive wine. People never minded paying for excellent cocktails and the best wine, and liquor was where the profits were anyway. Now he was ready to add an eighth location, the first in Montana, right here in Marietta, right in the old bookstore.

"Excuse me, I think I'm turned around," a young woman said, approaching him on the street. Her purple knit cap was pulled down low on her forehead, and her arms bundled across her chest. Her coat didn't look quite adequate for a Montana winter, and her cheeks were blotchy from the cold. "I was told there are several places serving dinner on Main. Grey's was mentioned, and then a diner."

Atticus pointed to a corner building across the street. "You're not far. Grey's is down one block, opposite side of the street, and the diner is down one more block, same side of the road."

"Grey's it is. Thank you," she answered, teeth chattering, before dashing across the street.

He watched her go, wondering idly if that was the Rachel Mills he was looking for, and then thought it unlikely that the one person he came to see, would be the one person asking him for directions. But he would see Rachel tomorrow, and all he had to do was convince her to sell, and he'd be on his way back to Houston. He wasn't worried about getting her to sell, either. Everyone had their price. Soon he'd know hers.

IT HAD TAKEN Rachel two flights to reach Bozeman from Orange County, and then a forty-minute drive in a rental car on a windy, snow-dusted road with hidden icy patches that caught her by surprise, making the drive a bit more white knuckled than she'd anticipated.

Admittedly, her knowledge of Montana was pretty much zilch, and she'd expected some mountains, but the freezing wind that tugged at her coat and blew her hair around her head as she stepped out of the car at the Bramble House caught her by surprise.

She was greeted warmly by the bed and breakfast's staff, and after a quick check-in was given an equally efficient tour before being shown upstairs to her room, and suggesting a few spots nearby for dinner, an easy walk to downtown if Rachel dressed warmly.

Bundled up, Rachel left Bramble House and walked two blocks to Second Street, crossing Crawford, and then Church Street, before coming to Main, and that was when she got confused. The street was quiet and dark, despite the pretty Christmas decorations festooned to the old-fashioned streetlamps. Nearly all of the buildings were two stories tall, and most were brick, or a mixture of brick and wood, with a Western façade.

She'd looked right and left, and then back toward the courthouse in the distant park, the dome of the courthouse bathed in light, the same light that made the peak of a big mountain standing sentry behind the town gleam. Which way was she supposed to go?

That was when she spotted the man on the corner, and thankfully he sorted her out and now she was stepping into Grey's Saloon, grateful to be out of the cold. A rugged-looking man in his thirties was working the bar and he nodded at her and told her to sit wherever she liked.

Rachel chose one of the empty tables as far from the jukebox as possible, and after peeling her coat and mittens and hat off, plucked the laminated menu from the condiment holder. She spotted the cobb salad and closed the menu. Done. White wine, a salad, and then tomorrow she'd find the bookstore, unlock the front door, and see what lay inside.

And then what?

What was she doing here? What was she thinking?

"That's a heavy sigh," the bartender said, now at her side.

She grimaced. "It's been a long day."

"What can I get you then?"

"The cobb salad and a glass of white wine. I'm not picky. Whatever you think is good works for me."

He nodded. "Make sure yourself comfortable and I'll be right back with the wine."

Her phone rang as the bartender walked away, and Rachel tugged off her scarf as she took the call. "Hello, Dad."

"You've arrived safely?" he asked.

"I have. Just sat down to dinner, too. There really is no need to worry about me."

"I still think you're making a terrible mistake."

"I'm not allowed to come see where Mom was from?"

"Of course you are, but this gift from Lesley. It's not practical. She has never been practical—"

"And yet Mom adored her."

"Just don't lose your head."

She refused to be provoked. "When have I ever done that?"

"I predict it's a crumbling building, overrun with silverfish," he said darkly.

"Haven't seen the bookstore yet, but happy to send a report tomorrow. Now, good night, Dad, and don't worry so much. Everything is going to be fine." Hanging up, Rachel peeled the rest of her layers off, piling them onto the bench seat next to her.

The woman at the booth in front of her turned around and flashed a friendly smile. "I'm sorry for eavesdropping," she said, tucking a long dark strand of hair behind her ear, "but I heard the word bookstore and my ears perked up. You're not Lesley's goddaughter, Rachel from Southern California, are you?"

Rachel blinked, surprised. "I am."

The woman reached over the top of the booth and extended her hand. "I'm Taylor Sheenan, the head librarian at Marietta's library, and a fellow book lover. So pleased to meet you."

Rachel shook hands thinking this wasn't the time to announce that she wasn't actually a book *lover*. If anything, she tended to tolerate books rather than embrace them. "Rachel Mills," she answered. "How did you hear about me?"

"Lesley and I have stayed in touch and she emailed me

last week to say that she'd gifted the store to her goddaughter Rachel from Southern California. And now here you are."

"Here I am," Rachel echoed uncomfortably.

"It will be wonderful to have the store open for Christmas."

"I'm not sure the store will be open for Christmas. I'm only here for a week or two."

"Oh." Taylor looked surprised, and then disappointed, and then she masked the disappointment with a polite smile. "Welcome to Marietta. Hope you enjoy your visit."

The bartender arrived with Rachel's salad and wine, but Rachel's appetite had faded, and she half-heartedly stabbed her fork into the salad.

She wasn't sure she was prepared for Marietta after all.

Fortunately dinner, and a good night's sleep, helped restore Rachel's equilibrium and she set off the next morning for Main Street again, stopping at Java Café for a coffee and scone before going to the bookstore.

She stood outside the store for a minute just taking it in. She'd stood on this very corner last night, getting directions from the man, and last night in the dark, she hadn't realized this was her store, and there was the painted wooden sign, hunter green with a pale gold outline. *Paradise Books.*

Even though the big Plateglass windows were shuttered on the inside, she felt a little thrill. This store was hers now. How crazy was that?

Eager now to see just what Lesley had given her, Rachel

unlocked the front door and turned on lights, delighted to discover her father was wrong. The brick building wasn't crumbling in any way, nor was it terribly musty after being closed for the past three plus years. Rachel set to work opening the wooden shutters, exposing the large expanse of glass and inviting the sun in. Outside it was a bright blue winter sky, and the streaming sun made the dust spirals look like swirling flecks of gold.

Thanks to the sun, Rachel could finally make out the window display, an ode to Valentine's Day, with red foil hearts and ivory cupid statues posed between popular romances from the nineteenth century—Jane Austen, Charlotte Bronte, Leo Tolstoy, Thomas Hardy. She wasn't sure *War and Peace*, or *Jude the Obscure*, would make anyone's list of top romance novels, but she'd give her godmother points for trying.

Rachel turned to face the interior of the store. So many leather-bound books. Such beautiful crown molding. Even the scattered upholstered armchairs looked elegant with their jeweled brocades and velvets. It was all so very different from her normal life. It was like being swept into a fairy tale, only this wasn't her fairy tale. This fairy tale was meant for someone else, someone more like Lesley, someone who'd treasure the books and history of the place.

Rachel was far too practical. She knew the value of a steady paycheck and a solid 401K plan. Small business owners didn't have that security, or retirement benefits.

Owning a used bookstore would provide even less security. No one wanted real books anymore. Everyone was decluttering and dumping their books, never mind books that were a half century old.

But what about those who actually lived here? Did anyone besides the librarian miss their old store? Or had everyone who read books gone digital? It made sense in a place like Marietta that was buried with snow months out of the year. Buying the newest bestseller from an online retailer would be the easy thing to do. Technology had changed the world and there was no going back.

But as Rachel stood in in the middle of this lovely light-filled space with the enormous windows and rich, dark shelves, she wished she was someone a little less practical. Someone who didn't live her life by numbers. Because the numbers were stacked against Paradise Books. The numbers, once added up, labeled this lovely old store a money pit.

The small bell on the front door jingled as it opened. Rachel wiped her dusty hands on the back of her jeans and turned to watch a tall, good-looking man in a sophisticated gray suit cross the threshold, his narrowed gaze skimming the interior before resting on her.

"Hello," she said. "Can I help you?"

"The lights were on. Wondered if you were open."

He was familiar, she thought, especially his voice, with that hint of drawl. She'd asked him for directions last night, hadn't she? "Not exactly," she answered, wondering if he recognized her. "I think you were the nice person who got me to Grey's for dinner last night."

His lips quirked. "I wondered," he said, his voice deep and firm.

Last night he'd merely been information. Today he was pure fascination. The man was tall and seriously good-looking—thick, wavy brown-black hair, straight brows, chiseled jaw—this kind of handsome didn't just walk through the door every day. At least, not her door.

Of course, she was wearing an old sweater and her favorite Levi's while he looked as if he'd just stepped from the pages of a men's magazine, his light gray dress shirt partially unbuttoned, exposing the column of his throat, hinting at a muscular chest. An unbuttoned collar wouldn't look out of place in California, but this was Montana and there was dirty snow piled up on the street corners and his bronzed throat and chest made it appear as if he'd just returned from the Maldives.

"So you're not open," he said.

"I'm just doing an inspection," she answered, "figuring out what's what."

"The store's been closed a long time."

"Almost three years," she said.

He nodded absently, as if he'd expected her to say that, and glanced around once more, his gaze studying the floor-to-ceiling bookshelves, shelves that filled up most of the downstairs. "You're the one I've come to see," he said after a moment, focusing on her again, his voice filling her with warmth.

"Me?"

"You're Rachel Mills."

He'd caught her off guard. How did he know her name? "Yes, I'm Rachel."

"The new owner of the bookstore."

He didn't say it as a question, but a statement, which made her wonder if everyone in Marietta knew about Lesley's gift to her. "Yes."

He extended his hand. "Atticus Bowen."

"Atticus?"

"My mother loved *To Kill a Mockingbird*."

She smiled reluctantly. "You're Southern, too."

"Texan. Houston."

"South Texas."

He laughed, and his teeth were very white, and his eyes very blue. "Lesley told me I'd find you here this week, so I flew in to meet you."

"You flew in to meet me?"

"Just arrived last night."

"So you haven't been impatiently waiting to purchase a book."

He gave her a lazy smile. "I've been impatiently waiting to make you an offer for all the books."

"You want all the books?"

"As well as the building."

"You want to own Paradise Books."

"I do."

If there was a category in one's yearbook for Least Likely to Own a Used Bookstore, this man would win it. "You love books?" she said in disbelief.

"That's probably an exaggeration. Books are fine, but I don't take them to bed with me."

She didn't know how it happened, but she heard him say, "take them to bed" and then mentally added the word, "naked," and then blushed, distracted, because Rachel didn't meet men and picture them naked, or in bed. But Atticus Bowen wasn't like any man she'd ever met.

"My mother always read in bed," he added helpfully. "Every night. She's the reader in the family."

Rachel really wished he'd stop mentioning beds. "And *she* wants the bookstore?"

"No."

Her confusion deepened. "If you don't love books, why this bookstore?"

"It's special," he said with a faint shrug.

She stared at him, fascinated. Everything about him exuded confidence, but it was that slight, mocking lift of his lips that held her attention. His mouth was sexy and confident. Dangerous. She'd heard men like this existed but had never met one in real life.

Rachel's real life was dominated by a calculator and spreadsheets. The people in her world were also good with numbers, and like her, they tended to be quiet, serious, average.

Atticus wasn't average.

For the first time in a long time, her life wasn't organized and predictable. She had no idea what would happen next.

"Does Lesley know you want to buy the bookstore?" she asked.

"She does."

"And what did she say?"

"That I should talk to you, as it's now yours."

Interesting, as well as convenient. Rachel's fingers curled into her palms, not sure she liked that everyone knew more about what was happening than her. Clearly, she needed to be looped in, fast. "How do you know her?"

"Friends of mine are friends with her."

"So no relation."

"None."

"And you've come all this way to meet me."

"I have."

"You must want this store badly."

The corner of his mouth tugged in a faintly rueful smile. "I do."

"This is an interesting development."

"So you're open to discussing the store with me?"

Her eyebrows arched. "Unless you're making a terrible offer, why wouldn't I be?"

"I would never make you a terrible offer. That would

disrespect your intelligence, and nothing good would come after that."

"True," she agreed.

CHAPTER TWO

SHE WASN'T WHAT he'd expected.

Based on Lesley's brief description, Atticus imagined someone of medium height and build, someone in a beige suit and sensible heels. Lesley's successful goddaughter would wear inoffensive pearls and her hair would be one of those bobs which conveyed nothing and yet everything.

But Lesley's goddaughter had thick, dark blonde hair gathered in a long ponytail, and she wore snug jeans, silver hoop earrings and a navy sweater with narrow white stripes. She looked fresh and young and nothing like an accountant. His gaze dropped to her feet. Vans. In winter.

Why was he surprised, though? She lived in Orange County, home of world-famous beaches and Disneyland. Of course she'd dress like a California girl. She *was* a California girl. And yet, when she opened her mouth she was clearly no fool.

"I don't know what your day looks like," he said, "but if you have some time, I'd like to sit down with you and discuss this properly. I've pulled some comps, put together some numbers, which should give you some context for the offer."

Her upper lip was generous, and slightly bow shaped, and it curved, matching the arch of her dark brown eyebrows. "Context is always useful." And then her blue-green eyes seemed to gleam. "I look forward to seeing your numbers."

He wasn't sure why he felt a whisper prickle of unease at the way she said "numbers." This was his game. He was the king of numbers. "My schedule is quite flexible. I'm meeting friends for dinner, but other than that, I have nothing else planned for today. Let me know what you prefer."

"Why don't we meet before your dinner and you can show me what you have?"

His eyes narrowed. That wasn't a double entendre, was it? But when he looked down into her face, her expression was perfectly innocent. Or perhaps it was just the smattering of freckles across the bridge of her nose that made her look innocent?

He wrestled the suspicion, suppressing the uncomfortable, unfamiliar sensation in his gut that she just might have seized the upper hand. "I'm staying at the Graff. We could meet there, or at the Depot."

"The Graff is great. I read they have a nice pub. I could meet you at five thirty."

"My dinner is at six as my friends have young children that go to bed early. Could you do five?"

"I could."

"See you then."

RACHEL'S PULSE THUDDED as she watched Atticus walk out of the bookstore.

Wow.

That was… he was… just wow.

And it wasn't just his whole beautiful face-body-charisma thing that intrigued her, but his interest in the store. What did he want with a bookstore? Rachel had run some numbers before she'd booked her flight, and she'd looked up real estate in the valley, as well as in neighboring Bozeman. There was very little commercial space available in Marietta, and land in Paradise Valley was at a premium. The area seemed to be thriving, and popular with the affluent who wanted to own a piece of the West. Was Atticus one of those hungry for his piece of the West?

She turned from the door, her gaze sweeping the tall bookshelves, and then the handsome stairs at the back, the stairs leading to the equally crammed second floor. Paradise Books had been named after Montana's famed Paradise Valley, and it gave Rachel pause that Lesley had options, and she could have sold the store to Atticus, but instead she'd gifted it to Rachel. Lesley wanted her to have the store. But why? Why did it mean so much to her, and even more importantly, could anyone—never mind Rachel—make it profitable?

She didn't know, but she pushed up the sleeves of her sweater, and began inspecting the shelves of books on both floors to get a lay of the land before heading into the back room to take a peek at the boxes filled with books. She opened one, and then another, and it looked as though every box consisted of vintage books and there were over a dozen boxes stacked in the storage room. Rachel didn't know if Lesley had bought the books from various customers, or perhaps she'd picked them up at estate sales or flea markets. Either way, these boxes of books had been sitting here for years, waiting for someone to go through them.

There was just so many, and the two floors of the store were filled with floor-to-ceiling shelves, and the shelves were crammed full. Where did one put the new books? And how was she supposed to decide what belonged on the shelves, and what should be discarded?

Obviously tattered paperbacks could go, and books that had duplicates already on the shelf would go, but what if one of the books had value? What if one of them was rare, or a first edition?

She exhaled hard, blowing her wispy bangs out of her eyes. She wasn't going to allow herself to get mired in doubts. Of course there would be a learning curve, but if she was practical and organized, and willing to do the research, she'd know what to do with the books. And she had some time right now. She was here for a week, maybe two. Why not tackle some of the books collecting dust in the storeroom? Sorting books didn't mean she had to keep the bookstore. In fact, sorting through the stock was probably an important first step to selling Paradise Books.

Footsteps sounded on the floorboards and a voice called out a deep hello.

"Hi," she said, popping out of the storeroom.

A tall, broad-shouldered cowboy in worn cowboy boots, dark Wranglers, and a heavy winter coat smiled at her, and removed his black cowboy hat. "Zane Nash," he said, extending his hand.

Rachel took his hand. "Rachel Mills," she answered, giving his hand a shake.

"I was given instructions to find you and introduce myself." His smile was wry. "I didn't realize you'd been here a few days already. I apologize for not coming by sooner."

"I only arrived last night," she corrected cheerfully. "Who gave you instructions?"

"Lesley."

"You know Lesley?"

"She was practically a second mom to me."

Finally someone who knew Lesley well. "It's really good to meet you. I have a million questions."

"I'll try to answer them if I can." His gaze swept the interior. "It's nice to see the store open again. It was closed far too long."

She felt a stab of guilt. "It's actually not open. I've just been doing some inventory, trying to see what's what."

Rachel hesitated. "Does Lesley have any family in Marietta anymore?"

He shook his head. "No. She was widowed young, before she had kids, and she never remarried."

"So how did she end up in Australia?"

"Her sister moved there, and she wanted to go see her. It was just supposed to be a visit but she decided she liked Queensland, and stayed. But she's been missed. She had a way of looking after others, and I'm grateful for all she did for me growing up. I got my love of books from her." He glanced past her to the boxes filling the storage room. "What's all that?"

"Books from the back room." She rubbed her forehead. "I'm not totally sure what to do with all of them. The bookstore is full, and yet there are hundreds more back here. What was she planning on doing with them?"

"Probably get them on the shelves when she returned from Australia."

"But where? The store is full."

"Lesley was creative when it came to making room for new books."

Creative or compulsive, Rachel wondered, even as a thought crossed her mind. "She didn't have a database for her books on the shelves, did she? Or any other formal record of her stock?"

"She has a set of binders beneath the counter with a list of books, but I don't know how up to date it is."

"Nothing on a computer?"

"Lesley didn't like computers. She wasn't very tech savvy. I tried to help her set up an online bookstore once, but she said it was impersonal. She loved hand selling and customer interaction. But she could have made some real money if her books were available online. She has a section of first editions in the tall glass cabinet near the counter, and she has a lot of specialty books that are probably collectibles, from nineteenth-century novels to the history of Montana and copper mining, etc."

"History and literature are not my area of expertise."

"No? But it's still impressive you're giving it a go. Paradise Books was practically my second home. I hated seeing it closed for so long."

She hadn't decided what she was going to do, but she didn't tell him that, thinking it wouldn't exactly endear her to him. "Did Lesley know how you felt about the bookstore?"

"Yes."

"Why didn't she give it to you then?"

Zane shrugged, unperturbed. "Maybe because she knew I wouldn't want it. It's one thing to enjoy spending time somewhere. It's another to make it your job."

Rachel thought of her office in Irvine, and the blinds she tended to keep closed against the bright California light to avoid glare on her computer screen, as well as the long, long hours she spent at her desk. If she'd known at the outset of her career what her days would be like, would she still have chosen it? "True."

"Lesley said you're a CFO in California."

"Not a CFO, just an accountant with a large accounting firm."

"She made it sound like you're quite successful."

"I suppose I am pretty good with a calculator."

"Unfortunately, you won't need a fancy calculator here. The bookstore business is kind of slow. Lesley didn't need the income. Her late husband left her in good shape. This was more of a passion than anything else."

She processed this a moment. "I wish I'd known her better. I've only met her a couple times in my life, and I feel a little guilty that she's given me something she loved so much."

His big shoulders shifted easily. "Don't feel guilty. Enjoy it."

Enjoy it.

Enjoy, she silently repeated after Zane left. But how? Rachel knew nothing about making a small business profitable, never mind a bookstore. And the thing was, she was far too careful with her money, to blow her savings on a losing proposition. It was risky using a couple of weeks of her vacation time on this visit to Marietta—the president at her company was far from thrilled that she was taking time off now—but she needed to figure out what she wanted, and the only way to do that, was evaluate all her options.

Which reminded her, it was growing late and unless she wanted to show up for drinks at the Graff Hotel covered in dust and dirt, she ought to lock up and head back to her room at the Bramble House for a shower and change of clothes.

THE GRAFF PROVED to be a surprisingly grand hotel from the turn of the century, built behind the old train depot, and from the same warm red brick that dominated Main Street. Festive wreaths decorated the front doors, and Rachel caught a whiff of fresh, fragrant pine as she stepped inside. A towering Christmas tree filled the lobby, and dark green garland with rich red velvet bows festooned the windows and doorways. It might be early December but it was already Christmas here at the historic hotel.

A uniformed bell captain pointed her to the pub where she spotted Atticus right away, seated at a corner booth. He rose as she approached the table and smiled. He'd changed into dark trousers and a black turtleneck sweater that hugged the planes of his muscular chest and emphasized his strong angular jaw now shadowed with five-o'clock stubble.

She'd thought him handsome in his three-piece suit but he was almost overwhelming now. He was so... fit... and confident, and that lazy, sexy smile of his was doing ridiculous things to her pulse, making her insides fluttery. That fluttery sensation in her middle didn't subside as she sat down and it was disconcerting to say the least.

"Good to see you," he said, his gaze meeting hers and holding.

His eyes, she realized, were blue, a light, piercing blue and they made her feel a little too warm, and a little too vulnerable. She made a show of peeling off her coat and removing her scarf and mittens.

"Good to be here," she said briskly, determined to regain her equilibrium. Just because Atticus was, well, Atticus, it didn't mean she couldn't manage to keep things purely professional. "It's my first time at the Graff. It's a really lovely old hotel."

"It looks particularly appealing now with the Christmas decorations."

"You've stayed here before."

"I'm friends with the owner, Troy Sheenan. He lets me stay in his suite whenever I'm in Marietta, and in return, I handle some legal things for him."

"Seems like a fair trade."

"He doesn't have me do much, so I think I've gotten the better end of the bargain."

The waitress arrived to take their drink order, and after she'd gone, Atticus asked her how she'd spent the afternoon.

She told him about the visit from Zane Nash, and the discovery that there were binders with records on books, but no electronic database. "The glass cabinet near the front is where she keeps the really valuable books, and apparently she has an excellent collection of books on Montana and the West. I haven't taken a look at those yet, but I did some dusting and cleaning and discovered an entire back room filled with boxes. There are so many books in there. I'm beginning to think that Lesley never met a book she didn't love."

He leaned back against the dark green leather booth. "Not everyone would view inheriting a store that size as a blessing."

"Especially a store that hasn't been introduced to the technology age. A store that size needs a database, not just to manage stock, but it would allow one to sell books online. I understand Lesley loved her customers, but relying on foot traffic limits sales."

"Especially during Montana winters," he agreed. "From what I gather, they begin in October and continue through April or May."

"It's certainly cold now."

"First time visiting Montana?"

"Second. Last time I was here I was in preschool. We came for a wedding. Apparently I was the flower girl." She saw his expression and shook her head. "I don't remember any of it."

"So what's your connection to Lesley, and Marietta?"

"My mom grew up here. She was born in Missoula but moved as a baby to Marietta. Her dad, my grandfather worked for the US Forest Service, and my grandmother was an elementary school teacher but she gave up teaching when they moved to Marietta. From what I gather, they were happy here, but then during my mom's senior year of high school, my grandfather was transferred to the Flathead Lake area, but my mother stayed behind, and lived with Lesley's family until graduation in June." Rachel looked across the pub to the fireplace where a fire crackled and popped. "My mom went to university in Missoula, and she met Dad there. He was earning his PhD and then when he got a job offer in Southern California, she followed him out."

"That's how you ended up in California."

"It's all I've ever really known."

"And your parents? What are they doing now?"

"Dad has retired and Mom"—she broke off, brow furrowing—"she passed away a number of years ago."

"I'm sorry."

"It was a long time ago."

"You're not that old."

"Just turned thirty."

"Again, not that old. It must have been a difficult loss."

For a moment, she couldn't speak, the weight on the past suddenly impossibly heavy and then she managed a small, nonchalant shrug. "I don't think about it." And that much was true. She hated thinking about her mom and the horrendous cancer that had taken three years to kill her. "Too much to do."

Their drinks had arrived and they made small talk for a

bit before Atticus drew a folder from his briefcase and slid it across the table. "I had the bookstore appraised eighteen months ago. I had it appraised again recently, just to make sure the numbers hadn't changed."

"And?"

"They've pretty much stayed the same."

"It will be interesting to see how your numbers compare to mine. I've done my homework, too."

"I expected you would," he answered, lips curving faintly. "Your profession is a lot like mine, time is money, and we probably both bill in fifteen minute increments."

"I hate having my time wasted."

"Something else we agree on." He drummed his fingers on the table. "What do you want out of this? What's the magic number to make this deal happen?"

"I'm not sure I have a magic number, at least not yet. This is all new to me, and I flew out to Montana on a research trip. I'm here to figure out what I want, and what the bookstore means, and the best moves for the future."

"That makes sense. Here's my bottom line—I want the bookstore, and I'll compensate you fairly, generously, but I also understand you need time. That's not a problem."

She took a sip from her glass and then looked at him, trying not to let his pretty face confuse her. She wasn't used to having drinks or interesting conversations with men like Atticus. "Why do you want the bookstore?"

"I want the building. I have a vision for it. And I don't

want to compromise that vision."

She noticed he said building this time, not store. "What do you want to do with it?"

"Turn it into a restaurant."

"A restaurant?"

"Location and setting are a big part of a restaurant's success. I think the bookstore's location on the corner makes it perfect for an upscale steak house."

"There are a lot of places you could do this in Montana—"

"I like Marietta. It reminds me a lot of Last Stand in Texas. Marietta draws folks from Bozeman and Livingston interested in a date night and fine dining, and then you have the seasonal traffic from tourists heading to Yellowstone."

"And all the books?"

"They'd find new homes," he said easily.

Too easily, she thought, tensing. And for the first time since meeting him this morning, she didn't trust him. He didn't care about the books. The books were in the way. He wanted the building and then he'd dispose of the books one way or another. In fact, for all she knew he'd simply have them carted to a dumpster.

Rachel felt rather queasy. She hadn't thought she cared about the books, either, but Lesley had taken care of them for years. One didn't just carelessly dispose of Lesley's books.

"I didn't need to travel to Montana to get comps on the building. I came here to understand the business," Rachel said slowly, carefully. "This was Lesley's passion for twenty plus years. It's a one-of-a-kind business. There aren't many independent bookstores in Montana, much less bookstores that have been in business in the same location since 1945."

His blue gaze met hers. "Which is why you'll see I'm making a significant offer."

She didn't look away, nor did she reach for the folder. She'd do that later when she was alone. For now, it was enough to know that he was serious about the bookstore. She should be relieved. She hadn't thought she wanted it, and the fact that there was a buyer, and a hungry buyer, should reassure her. He was giving her the perfect solution to a financial nightmare, and she should be excited... even grateful. Why wasn't she?

Didn't she want to return home and resume the life she knew?

Again, her tiny office with the darkened blinds flashed through her mind, and this time the memory made her feel a little sick. She'd sacrificed so much—travel, fun, friends, relationships—and maybe in the past she could justify the decision to pour everything into her work, but not anymore. She wasn't happy at Novak & Bartley. She hadn't been happy for a long time.

Maybe that was why she wasn't in a hurry to sell Paradise Books. The store teased new beginnings, and new opportunities. She knew what waited in Irvine. Marietta was a brand-new adventure. Was it time to try something different? Was she ready for a change?

Atticus studied her intently. "You don't know what you want to do, do you?"

"My head says I can't possibly keep it."

"But your heart…"

She laughed grimly. "Oh, no, I don't ever listen to my heart." She saw his expression and made a face. "I don't trust it. Hearts and feelings are unpredictable. I prefer numbers and equations; those can be relied on."

"If you know that about yourself, then you know you're not going to keep the store, because it's not going to be profitable."

"What if there was a way to make it profitable?"

"I have no doubt that if anyone could do it, it would be you, but tell me honestly, would you really give up your job and your career to make a go of a used bookstore in Paradise Valley?"

She sighed and rubbed at the bridge of her nose. "Put like that, no. But at the same time, there is a lot for me to think about. I only recently inherited the store. It's still all so new to me. I'm still getting used to the idea that I own a business in Montana."

His dark head inclined. "I respect that."

She waited for him to say more, but he didn't, and she exhaled, feeling some of the tightness in her shoulders ease. "The easy thing to do would be to sell to you. I could cash out and fly home and never have to think about the store again, but that seems so unfair to do to Lesley. If she'd wanted to sell it to you, why didn't she?"

"I think if she'd gotten to know me, she would have liked me."

"I don't think this had to do with you per se, but the store itself. I think she wanted me to have it... but why? That's the part that's keeping me up at night. Why did she give it to me? I don't know, and that's what I need to find out."

He said nothing, and his silence felt like judgment.

"You think I'm making a mistake," she said.

"No," he answered, surprising her. "I think you're wise. You have options. You should explore them."

"Even if it means you don't get what you want?"

"I'm not worried. I play the long game."

Rachel didn't remember the last time she felt so overwhelmed by the need to make decisions, and yet for the life of her, she wasn't ready to decide anything. "I just need time," she added.

"Then take it."

"But you've flown here to meet me. You must be in a rush—"

"I'm not."

She gave him a searching glance.

He shrugged. "I've been talking to Lesley for the past eighteen months about the bookstore. I can certainly give you whatever time you need." The antique clock on the wall chimed. Atticus glanced up at it and then grimaced. "Has it been an hour already?"

"How is that possible?"

He reached for his wallet and she stopped him. "I've got this. Don't be any later than you already are."

"I can put it on my room."

"I'm going to stay and have dinner, so go. Don't keep your friends waiting."

He rose and reached for his coat. "How long will you be in town?"

She'd bought a one-way ticket because she didn't know how long she'd want to be here. "Not exactly sure. You?"

"Taylor is hoping I'll stay through the stroll, which happens next weekend. It's supposed to be a big deal."

"I'm sure we'll bump into each other sooner or later."

Rachel remained in the Graff pub after Atticus had gone, going through the folder he'd given her. She read everything in the file, too, including all the fine print as she nibbled on the skinny salted fries. He was right, his offer wasn't just generous, it was dazzling. That kind of money would go a long way toward her retirement nest egg, especially if she invested the money wisely—which of course, she always did.

But for the first time in forever, she didn't feel reassured by her investments, or her careful, thoughtful planning. What good would a lavish retirement be, if she were all alone?

"WHAT IS SHE like?" Troy asked, rinsing the last of the big pans before setting it on the counter to dry.

Atticus reached for it, just as he'd reached for the other dishes that Troy had hand-washed once the dishwasher was full. "Smart. Savvy. Rather fascinating."

"A fascinating accountant? There's a first," Troy answered, turning the water off.

"What Atticus isn't telling you is that Rachel is very pretty," Taylor said, returning to the kitchen after putting the kids to bed. Usually Troy helped read the stories and tuck them in, but tonight Taylor tackled the bedtime routine while Troy and Atticus managed the dishes.

"I've met her," Taylor added, putting away the assorted pots and pans. "We didn't talk long, but I liked her. I hope she'll keep the bookstore open."

Troy smiled. "Even though Atticus wants it?"

"He doesn't have to turn the bookstore into a steak place," she answered, shooting Atticus a mock severe glance. "He could find a different spot. There are lots of places vacant in Livingston right now. Why not one of those buildings?"

"But I want to be in Marietta, near you," Atticus answered, snapping his dish towel at Taylor as she passed him.

"I'd like you to be here, too. Just not in my bookstore."

"Your bookstore?" he retorted, looking from her to Troy. "Are you making an offer as well?"

Taylor and Troy exchanged glances. "Not yet," Taylor

replied lightly, "but we've discussed the store, and Troy knows that I feel it's important for Marietta to have its own bookstore."

Atticus leaned against the counter, arms folding over his chest. "I'd think you'd want everyone to take advantage of your library."

"I love Marietta's library, but I can also want to support our indie bookstore. In my mind, you can never have enough books."

"But who are the customers for the bookstore? Paradise Books is almost all vintage books."

"Lesley specialized in collectibles—her children's collection makes my mouth water—but she always carried new books, too. Maybe not as many as a chain bookstore would, but she'd special order titles for her customers. Whenever I wanted something, whether it was a cookbook or the most recent *New York Times* bestseller, she'd place an order, and I'd have it within a week."

"But you could do that yourself online and have it sooner."

"I could, but that wouldn't support our local businesses, and I value our small business owners."

Atticus didn't like how Taylor was making him feel like a bad guy. He wasn't a bad guy. He could be a tough negotiator, but he was always fair. It was important to him to be fair, and one of the reasons he'd switched from litigation to real estate law. "I didn't set my sights on a thriving business.

The bookstore has been closed for three years."

Taylor plucked the dish towel from his hands and hung it on the towel rack tucked inside the sink cabinet doors. "Now we have a chance for it to be open again."

Troy had been silently following the back and forth between his friend and wife and he cleared his throat. "And that decision rests squarely with Rachel. It will be interesting to see what she chooses to do."

"It will," Atticus replied. "And on that note, I should say good night. Thank you for dinner," he said, giving Taylor a hug. "It was delicious as always, and you know how much I enjoy my time with your family."

"I'll walk you out," Troy said, getting Atticus's coat from the house's hall closet.

It was a clear night and stars glittered overhead. Colorful lights glowed on the houses lining Bramble.

"I need to put our lights up," Troy said, glancing up at his ornate two-story Victorian painted a soft sage green with a paler green trim. "I'm finding it hard to get in the spirit this year. It's always hard when Thanksgiving is so late in November. This year I'm still thinking turkeys and pilgrims instead of Christmas decorations."

"Your kids are certainly excited about getting the tree this weekend."

"I'll be excited when we bring the ornaments down from the attic. I'm just not there yet." Troy hesitated. "Taylor is right, though, Atticus. Not everyone in Marietta will want to see the bookstore go. You might get some pushback."

"I'm expecting some," Atticus answered calmly, because it was true. In a place like Marietta change could be hard, and there were those who wanted everything to stay the same... even when it didn't work anymore.

"What if Rachel does choose to sell... only not to you?"

"Is there someone else interested in that spot?" Atticus looked at Troy. "Are you possibly interested?"

"No, and I can't speak for Taylor, but I don't see how she could remain at the library and own the store, and raise four children."

"You only have three—" Atticus broke off as he saw Troy's crooked smile. "She's pregnant?"

"Almost four months, but we haven't announced it yet. She had a miscarriage last year so we're trying to keep it quiet until we're comfortable with everyone knowing the news."

"Congratulations, though. I'm happy for you. You have an amazing family."

"We own a big house so we figured we might as well fill it up." Troy's smile faded. "And not to be a negative Nancy, but I'd hate for you to pin all your hopes on the bookstore, not when you have other options."

"I respect that. I also respect that Taylor really loves the bookstore. We need people like her who care about books, and promote literacy. But let's be honest, this community survived just fine the past three years. People found a way to buy their books, probably heading out of town to Walmart or Target, or choosing to purchase online. It's one thing to love the idea of something—in this case, a charming Main Street bookstore—but it's another to make it self-sufficient. Paradise Books is not going to pay for itself. Whoever takes it on needs to be prepared to bleed red for quite some time."

"This Rachel Mills might surprise you."

Atticus pictured Rachel with her blonde ponytail, Levi's jeans, and funky Vans and knew that Troy was right. "She's already surprised me," he said gruffly. "She's not at all who I thought she'd be."

Troy lifted a black eyebrow. "You don't make that sound like a good thing."

"It'd be easier if she was who I expected. Now I'm just conflicted."

Chapter Three

Main Street was still asleep when Rachel drove to the bookstore early the next morning, fortified with coffee, her laptop, and her phone—which she intended to use as a Wi-Fi hot spot later since the old brick building didn't have internet—and a large quantity of cleaning supplies.

A few cars were on Main Street, and warm yellow shone from within the Java Café and Main Street Diner, but nearly all of the other stores and restaurants were dark. Unlocking the front door of the bookstore, she flicked on the overhead light and stood on the threshold, soaking it in, appreciating it even more this morning, and how Lesley had thoughtfully placed upholstered armchairs here and there, creating inviting spaces to sit and read.

The irony hit her all over again—she didn't get the promotion, but she did get a bookstore in Montana. It would have been laughable if she hadn't poured herself into her career, working tirelessly to become Novak & Bartley's first female partner. She saw what was required and she took on more accounts, and asked for more responsibility, and worked longer hours, earning the firm more money, certain that eventually her loyalty would be noticed and rewarded.

But that hadn't happened, and she'd been at Novak & Bartley for almost eight years. If she wasn't going to be promoted now, when would she?

Was it time to choose a different path? Time to set new goals?

Was there a future here in this corner bookstore?

After tying her hair into a knot on top of her head, Rachel dusted, and then swept and mopped, tackling the downstairs before moving to the second floor. Once all the wood gleamed and the store smelled fresh from the lemon polish, she noticed how the spines of the books added warmth, color, and texture.

Rachel hadn't ever spent much time thinking about bookstores until now. In her mind, they were just another store, and she'd been raised to take advantage of the library, and not spend money on books of her own, but knowing all of this—the books, the reading nooks, the high ceilings and crown moldings—filled her with a pleasure she hadn't expected.

Curious now to see the attic apartment, Rachel unlocked the door in the back room, and climbed the stairs, turning on lights as she went. At the top of the landing she discovered the stairwell divided the apartment in half, with a living room and kitchen at one end, and a bedroom and bathroom at the other. Sky lights had been cut into the roof, and an oval window above the bed had a stunning view of the Gallatin Range and Copper Mountain.

Someone had been clever enough to turn the narrow hallways into functional space, with one side having built-in closets and dressers, and the other side bookshelves and a small desk. A framed bulletin board hung above the desk, but the steep slope of the rafters meant there wasn't tremendous headspace. Fortunately, Rachel wasn't tall and she liked the coziness of the apartment, and thought she could be quite comfortable here once she took her dust cloth and broom to everything. She'd thoroughly enjoyed Bramble House—they served a lovely, hot breakfast every morning—but this was free, and she hated spending money when it wasn't necessary, so she'd give the bed and breakfast notice that tonight would be her last night with them.

Using her phone, she created a new to-do list, making notes of what was in the apartment, and what she'd need to purchase. Happily, she discovered linens, quilts, and pillows in zipper storage bags tucked in a cedar-lined stairwell closet. Opening the bags, she sniffed the linens and they smelled of lavender and vanilla thanks to little sachets tucked between all the layers. The small kitchen had everything she'd need from dishes and silverware, to baking sheets and pots and pans. All she really needed was to grocery shop and carry everything up.

With one last glance at her notes, she returned downstairs and went through everything behind the front counter, including the binders Zane had mentioned. Lesley's organizational system was baffling. The book titles appeared to be added as Lesley purchased them, and then marked off as the books sold, all done in Lesley's neat penmanship, but there was no alphabetical list of titles, or organization by subject matter.

Opening her computer, Rachel created a brand-new spreadsheet entitled Paradise Books—Used Book Catalog, and then retrieved a box of books from the back room, and picked up the first hardback, a dusty caramel color embossed in hunter green, *The Oregon Trail*. Opening the book cover, she typed the title, author's name and 1912 copyright into Google search and immediately the book popped up, editions being sold by different bookstores, and the editions ranged from four hundred dollars for a signed first edition, to forty-four dollars for a book almost identical to the one resting on the counter next to her computer.

She was surprised that the book was worth as much, but also aware it'd take a unique buyer to purchase the book for forty-four dollars. "You're rather special," she said to the book, creating her first spreadsheet entry by inputting the title, the author name, the year published, the book's condition, and then placing the book in a "keep" stack.

She reached for the next book, a small relatively slim blue hardbound book titled *Wilderness Ways*. It was published in 1901, and an inscription was written on the first page, *For my dear Stanley, merry Christmas. With love from your grand-*

mother, Evelyn Camfield December 25, 1902.

Rachel felt a little pang as she traced the delicately penned inscription with the tip of her finger. The letters were slanted, and somewhat quivery, and yet she could feel the love in the inscription. But typing the book's info into the search engine, she discovered that the book wasn't valuable, with prices ranging from just ten dollars to sixteen, and yet, to her, the book took on significance as, once upon a time, it had meant something to someone. She closed the cover and studied the book a long moment before adding the book to her database.

Rachel didn't know how long she'd been working, sitting on the stool, hunched over her computer on the counter, going through books, researching history and value, when the front door opened, making the little bell ring.

It was Atticus coming through the door and today he'd dressed more appropriately for the cold by at least wearing a jacket.

"Good morning," she said as he closed the door behind him.

"It's the afternoon," he answered. "It's nearly two."

"Is it? I had no idea." She sat up taller and stretched.

"What are you doing?" he asked, leaning on the counter, invading her space.

She ought to be annoyed. Instead she felt a quickening of her pulse, her heart beating a little faster. She didn't want to respond to him but energy seemed to crackle around him, making everything come to life. "Trying to sort through books and figure out which ones to keep, and when I find a keeper, I add it to the spreadsheet I just created. But the storage room is filled with books. It's taken me a couple hours and I've gone through only one box of the books in the back room. I still have another twelve boxes to go."

"Progress is progress."

"Thanks for the encouragement."

The corner of his mouth lifted. His expression warmed as his gaze met hers. "Find any keepers?"

That half smile of his had her heart racing. Did Atticus have any idea that he was playing havoc with her sense of control? "These," she said, touching a tall pile. "And those are the rejects," she added, indicating a much smaller stack.

"You're saving most."

"So far, but there might be boxes that are just yellowed paperbacks."

He glanced around the store with the shelves of warm, colorful spines. "Lesley's books are in good shape. I have a feeling she'd only acquire books she thought might have value."

"She does have a lot of good books," she answered. "In one of the boxes, I found a set of *The Five Little Peppers*, and each one is worth fifty dollars or more, and she has six from the series, and they're all in excellent shape."

"What about this one?" he asked, picking up a mustard-yellow book with red-and-black art. "*The Red Cross Girls?*"

"That one isn't worth very much. Maybe seven dollars."

"But you have it in the keeper stack."

"I know, because look," Rachel said, opening the cover and turning to the first page where it had been inscribed. *"To Bessie, on your twelfth birthday, from Grandma Sterba."*

"And this one?" he asked, holding up a battered copy of *Little Men*. "The cover has come completely off. The pages are falling out."

She leaned over and opened the book. "It's to Bessie again," she said.

"Who is Bessie?" he asked.

"I don't know, but most of the books in this box seem to have belonged to Bessie—or Elizabeth—and they were all well-loved. A few of them more loved than others."

"Surely you can let go of the ones that were overly loved."

Rachel returned the copy of *Little Men* to the tall stack and nudged them so they were perfectly straight. "Elizabeth saved these since she was a little girl, and she took good care of them. It's hard to be ruthless now."

"But it's practical," he answered. "You can't keep everything. There isn't room for them all."

She said nothing, because he was right. She couldn't keep everything, and if she did sell the store to him, he'd keep nothing.

"You're getting attached, aren't you?" he asked, but his tone was kind.

"I don't know. I do worry I've opened a can of worms. It might have been better to have stayed home and played ostrich. The store's been closed for years. I could have left it the way it was."

"You can still do that."

She looked at the books on the counter, and then her laptop screen showing the new database. She'd researched for hours and after researching, had input twenty some books. The store had thousands more. Bringing the store into the electronic age would be a labor of love, and for someone with a full-time job, nearly impossible. "I want to do right by Lesley."

"She'd want you to do what makes you happy."

Rachel bit her lip, not knowing that answer, either.

"Don't be frustrated," he said. "You're doing great."

"Am I?"

"I think so. You just need some fresh air to help clear your head. Have you been out today? Did you go get lunch?"

"No, and now that you mention it, I am hungry, and grumpy," she added with a grimace.

"If you feel like walking, we could hit a place on Main Street, or, if you thought you could wait another thirty minutes, I could take you to a little place in Paradise Valley, and you'd have a chance to see some of Montana's magnificent scenery."

"Magnificent scenery is the way to go."

"Grab your coat and lock up. We're going for a drive."

ATTICUS'S CAR WAS a four-wheel drive SUV, and he drove Highway 89 with the same confidence he did everything else. She realized almost right away she was in good hands and little by little she relaxed, or at least, she tried to relax but part of her was all too aware of Atticus next to her. She'd been around other men who were tall, and she'd been around men who were powerful, but Atticus exuded strength and a very sexy masculinity that made her feel a little tingly and nervous. It was disconcerting, too, as she worked daily with men and none of them made her skin feel sensitive and her pulse race. The truth was, she didn't even know most of them existed.

Breathe. Inhale. Exhale. And again.

Rachel rested her elbow on the door, put her chin in her hand and watched the world go by. It was a beautiful world, too, with jagged snow-covered peaks silhouetted against a brilliant blue sky. The Yellowstone River curved through the valley floor, paralleling the two-lane road, the icy blue water a contrast to the snow dusted riverbank.

Pastures covered the hills, with cattle in some and horses in others. Big old barns of weathered wood were tucked next to old homesteads, while big, luxurious new construction dwarfed leafless poplar trees. It was all interesting, though, and new, and it'd look different in spring and fall, when the hills were green and gold.

"You okay?" Atticus asked, breaking the silence.

She looked at him, took in that rugged profile of his and nodded faintly. "Yeah."

He shot her a side glance. "You're pretty quiet."

"Just trying to relax." She wrinkled her nose, expression rueful. "It's not something I do often, or do well."

"I can turn around."

"*No*, please don't. I'm enjoying this, I really am." Glancing back out the window she spotted a sign. *Gallagher Christmas Tree Farm ¼ mile*. Rachel felt a prick of curiosity. She'd never been to a Christmas tree farm before. Did one cut your own tree down, or did they do it for you?

"Have you ever been there?" she asked, pointing to the next sign reading *Turn Here for Gallagher Tree Farm*.

"No," he answered. "But a lot of people from Marietta come out here to get their trees. I think Troy and Taylor bring their kids here."

"We go to tree lots where I live. The lots are all asphalt, usually on an empty corner or in some big parking lot."

"We do that in Texas, too."

"I haven't actually had a real tree in oh—years. In fact, I can't even remember the last time I put up a tree. Just seemed wasteful."

"Too much money?"

"I'm not home enough to enjoy decorations. I spend most of my time at the office."

"Your boyfriend is good with that?"

Amused, she met his gaze. "Relationships fall under the

Christmas tree category—there simply isn't time."

"So no significant other?"

"Not in a while, no."

"How long?"

She wasn't about to admit it been over a year, or that she'd given up dating because she was tired of men criticizing her for being a workaholic, when most of them she'd dated put in nearly the same hours she did. For some reason, men who worked hard were admired, but it wasn't an attractive quality in a woman. "You answer first," she retorted.

"Me?"

"Yes. Come on. Fair is fair. Are you seeing someone? Is it serious? When do you plan on getting married? How many kids do you think you'll have?"

He laughed, and the deep husky sound filled the inside of the car. "You're ruthless."

"*You're* ruthless. I was just happy to sit and let you drive."

"True," he answered. "And if you're happy, I'm happy."

Her gaze slid slowly over his handsome profile again, a strange warmth filling her. "I'm good," she said softly, before turning her attention to the landscape. And she was good. She couldn't remember the last time she did anything like this, and yet it felt familiar, and comforting, in the best sort of way.

"We used to go on drives when I was a little girl," she said after a long moment. "My dad isn't a material person, but when I was growing up he had a baby-blue 1960 Cadillac. He loved that car. The car was a boat, with fins and a bullet grill and blue-and-white bench seats. On weekends he'd wash his car, fill it with gas, and we'd drive from Irvine to Laguna, where we'd cruise the Pacific Coast Highway. Dad would play Elvis and Johnny Cash, and I'd sit in the back seat with my hair blowing everywhere and the sun in my eyes, singing 'Ring of Fire.'" She swallowed hard around the lump in her throat. "Those drives were my idea of happiness. Sunshine and blue sky, the road and the wheels of the car..." Her voice faded and she drew a slow breath, fighting the emotion. "I don't think I've been for a proper drive since Mom died," she added huskily.

"What happened to the Cadillac?"

"Dad sold it my first year of college." She shrugged uncomfortably. "He said he did it to pay bills, but I was living at home during school. UC Irvine was a public university. Tuition wasn't that much of a burden. He sold it because the car reminded him too much of Mom."

ATTICUS HEARD RACHEL'S soft sigh and he glanced at her, concerned, but he couldn't read her mood. She seemed to have mastered the calm, neutral, no emotion expression a little too well. "Did your dad ever remarry?" he asked.

"No. Have there been women? Probably. But he's never introduced me to anyone, or moved anyone into our house."

She suddenly wrinkled her nose. "Let me also clarify that I don't still live at home. I have my own place. I bought it four years ago. I just meant that, so far, Dad's never moved anyone into the family house."

"Would you mind if he did?"

She didn't immediately answer and he could see from her furrowed brow that she was thinking. "No, I don't suppose so. I want him happy."

"You don't think he's happy?"

Rachel's shoulders twisted. "I don't know. We don't talk about… feelings… in my family." She drew a quick breath and added more lowly, "And we don't talk about Mom, or that she's gone. After the funeral, we just kind of… moved on."

A heavy beat of silence followed her words and when Atticus glanced at her, he saw the grief in her eyes and a quiver in her lower lip, a quiver she ended by ruthlessly biting into her lip. She was wrong, he thought. They hadn't moved on, and he suspected, Rachel still struggled with the loss.

Atticus shifted his hand on the steering wheel, fingers tightening around the wheel as it crossed his mind that maybe this drive was a mistake. Being near Rachel was increasingly problematic. Rachel wasn't his type and yet he felt protective of her and that was the last thing he wanted to feel. He wanted the bookstore, not Rachel.

He wanted to open a restaurant, not pursue a relationship. If he wanted female company, he knew where to find it, and the women he dated understood that he wasn't interested in a wife, or commitments, at least not yet. He'd grown up in a loving family and had always assumed he'd marry and settle down, but that had been before, when he'd been a brash litigator and he thought the world was his oyster. After switching careers, he'd been forced to confront his weaknesses, and he'd realized that yes, one day he might make a good husband and father, but he wasn't there yet. In the meantime, he surrounded himself with fashionable socialites who were easy and fun, women who appreciated expensive dinners and were delighted by A-list parties. His girlfriends weren't demanding, usually happy just to dress up and go out and be seen. He tried to imagine Rachel in the VIP section of one of the swanky clubs, but it was impossible to picture her gyrating on the dance floor, or sprawled across his lap at their table, texting and taking selfies while downing bottles of champagne.

"Why accounting?" he asked abruptly.

Her slim shoulders lifted and fell. "I was always really good at math. President of the math club in high school, honors math and science courses. I've just always liked numbers. They make sense to me."

"There are a lot of things you could do with math besides accounting. Economist, financial planner, investment analyst, statistician—"

"Professor," she interrupted. "I know. My dad was an econ professor, but the difference is, he enjoyed working with people. I like to work alone. And I like accounting. I like the precision, I like the research, I like tax law. It's just a good fit for my personality."

"As an accountant you work with people."

"Very little, compared to some of the other careers you mentioned, and I like not being dependent on other people to do my job. People, in my experience aren't predictable and orderly."

He smiled faintly. "This is true."

"And numbers have never let me down," she added.

"But people have," he said quietly.

She looked at him, expression sober. "Lately they have, yes."

"Want to talk about it?"

"No."

Interesting, he thought, but didn't push. Instead he asked more questions. "Did you study accounting in college?"

"I did, and was offered an internship with Novak & Bartley on graduation, with the understanding that I'd take the Uniform CPA exam at the end of a year, and if I passed the exam, I'd be offered a full-time position. I've been with Novak & Bartley ever since."

"So what do you do for fun?"

"Define fun," she retorted.

"Dressing up, cutting lose, going out, drinking, dancing." He paused. "Do you do any of that? Do you ever go dancing?"

Her forehead furrowed. "Dance? Like... night clubs, or line dancing?"

"Yes. Do you have a favorite club in LA? Or a venue where you go listen to music?"

She gave him an incredulous look. "And who would I do this with? My fellow accountants?"

"Surely you have a group of girlfriends—"

"Oh right, my posse." And then she rolled her eyes. "I'm not Taylor Swift."

"You have to have friends."

"Have I complained that I'm lonely? Because I'm not. I'm busy. I work hard."

"I don't doubt it. But what do you do in your free time?"

"I thought we covered this already. I don't have a lot of free time. I work."

"Even on weekends?"

"If I'm not in the office on Saturday, I'm pouring over files on my dining room table."

"Why?"

"What do you mean why? To get ahead, you have to put in the hours, which is what I've been doing."

"So, you are being rewarded for your hard work."

There was a slight pause before she answered. "Yes," she said quietly.

It was only a brief hesitation but it was enough to get his attention. He'd been a very good trial lawyer at one point in time—back before the case that changed everything—and he might have given up the court room, but he could still read people well.

She wasn't being entirely truthful with him, but why should she? They weren't friends. She owed him nothing. He wasn't even sure why he cared, or why he'd been so compelled to get her out of the stuffy store for a change of scenery. Inserting himself into her life would just complicate negotiations. From now on, he had to be more careful. More distance, less familiarity.

He pulled off the highway a short time later in Emigrant where they'd have lunch at the barbecue restaurant Troy had taken him to on one of Atticus's first visits to Crawford County. Over ribs and brisket he told her about the Sheenans, mentioning that Taylor said she'd met Rachel a couple nights before.

At first Rachel was puzzled, but when he added that Taylor was the head librarian Rachel's expression cleared. "Yes, I do remember her. I talked to her at Grey's Saloon. She seemed very excited that the bookstore might be open again."

"Zane Nash said the same thing, didn't he?" Atticus said, trying to keep all emotion from his voice, not wanting to influence her one way or the other.

"He did," she agreed. "But I'm not actually opening the bookstore. I'm just looking at the records and doing some research."

Atticus wiped his sticky fingers off on the paper napkin and pushed his plate back. "Maybe you should open it while you're here. If you're going to be in town a couple weeks, run it like a real business and see what kind of response you get. It might help clarify things."

She studied him for a moment. "You think Taylor and Zane are exceptions to the rule."

He shrugged. "I think people are sentimental about the bookstore, yes, but the people who are sentimental aren't the ones who will be dipping into their savings account to pay for upkeep and expenses. We both know that store is not going to pay for itself. I predict it'll be a nonprofit for years to come."

Rachel didn't smile. In fact, she looked downright annoyed. "I don't know if it'd struggle for *years*. It might be a rough first year, but there are ways to shore up the income. Carry more new books, add a selection of cards and gifts, lease part of the space to another business."

"Like who?"

"An artist, maybe."

"So you'd tear out bookshelves and create room for art?"

She glared at him. "You were so encouraging and supportive earlier, and now you're just being mean."

"I'm not being mean. I'm being honest, and practical. Paradise Books, in my opinion, is going to be a massive financial drain, but that's just my opinion, so don't listen to me. It's your bookstore, as well as your opportunity to prove me wrong. I'd love for you to prove me wrong."

"Oh, would you?" she retorted grimly, a flash of temper in her blue-green eyes.

He welcomed the flare of temper, reassured by the blaze of heat in her expression. She wasn't quite as cool and controlled as she liked to pretend. "Open the doors. Make it a trial run. You might discover you love owning a bookstore. But you also might discover that it's not for you."

"That's a great idea," she said. "I'm here for a couple weeks. Why not open the store tomorrow?"

"Can't wait to see what you'll do with the place."

Rachel crumpled her napkin and tossed it onto her plate before standing up. "Since it looks like I have work to do, I'd like to head back."

He rose as well. "You're not angry, are you?"

"Why would I be angry?" she asked, shoving her arms into coat sleeves. "I'm opening my bookstore just in time for the holidays. I couldn't be more excited."

Chapter Four

Rachel seethed on the drive back to town, and was still seething when she went to bed that night, her last night at Bramble House. Fortunately, by the time she woke up, her anger had melted away, replaced by quiet determination.

She'd show Atticus he was wrong. She'd show him that Paradise Books wasn't doomed, nor was it a sentimental relic of the past, but rather it was a business that was still vital to the community.

After checking out of the bed and breakfast, she drove to the nearest grocery store and bought some basic supplies, and then headed to Paradise Books to settle in. This morning she looked at the store with new eyes. She wasn't going to let herself be negative. For the next ten days she'd focus on opportunity and possibility, and with Christmas right around the corner, why couldn't she get some strong holiday sales? She just needed to fix up the windows and create some attractive displays and before long everybody would be coming in and buying things, and making spirits bright.

Her gaze went to the big windows where, until yesterday,

a Valentine's Day display had filled the windows for three years. Clearly it was time for a new display, a Christmas display, something inviting so folks would want to come in. She'd need to locate the Christmas books. Surely Lesley had Christmas books. Rachel would just need to find them.

What else?

Some festive decorations. Something easy, though, and inexpensive, because her practical side hadn't gone dormant, and was whispering to her even now that a used bookstore wasn't practical, not in a technology-driven age, but at the same time, she didn't have to give that little voice free reign. She'd spent her life being rational, and lately she'd been feeling...

Frustrated.

Bored.

Dissatisfied.

And now, for the first time in years, she felt excitement. *Eagerness.* Okay, there was a fair amount of anxiety mixed in with the other emotions, but that was to be expected. Rachel was a perfectionist and while she didn't know the first thing about running a store, she could learn.

After searching the shelves, she only found a half dozen Christmas titles, but three in each window was better than nothing.

At nine o'clock, she walked down to the Mercantile on Main Street and bought four of their large red poinsettias, two for each of the big Plateglass windows, along with two boxes of miniature white lights, and two nine foot extension cords. She carried everything back to the bookstore, removed the lights from the packaging and laid them out in a straight line along the base of the window, and then added the flowers and then took the books she'd found, putting three in each side.

At ten o'clock on the dot, she turned the sign over in the door, switching from *Closed* to *Open* for the first time in almost three years. Rachel felt a little frisson of excitement as she stepped behind her counter, eager to see what the day would bring.

THE DOORBELL JINGLED as it opened and Rachel looked up from her computer with a smile, ready to greet her first customer. But it wasn't a customer, it was just Atticus back to torment her some more.

Her smile faded. "Can I help you?" she asked stiffly.

"I brought you a celebratory scone from Java Café," he said, carrying a paper bag and tray with coffees to the counter. "Not sure which you'd prefer so I bought all three varieties, pumpkin, lemon, and cranberry."

She refused to be charmed. He'd pretty much ruined yesterday afternoon and she wasn't ready to forgive him. "That wasn't necessary."

"It's your first day in business. Of course we need to celebrate."

She lifted her chin and squarely met his gaze. "If I celebrated, it would be with a friend. You, Atticus Bowen, have firmly been placed in my nemesis category."

"Is that a category on your spreadsheet?"

"I'm astonished you even have friends. You're rather unbearable."

He grinned lazily and plucked a coffee from the paper tray and placed it in front of her. "Pumpkin spice latte to sweeten you up."

"Atticus."

"Yes, Rachel?"

"Why are you here?"

"I can't possibly be happy for you? Excited to share in your grand reopening?"

Rachel prided herself on her self-control but she had a sudden vision of herself dumping her pumpkin spice latte over Atticus's head and watching it drip down his handsome face to collect in his sweater. Just the thought alone gave her immense pleasure. "In that case, have a look around. Maybe there's a book or two that will catch your eye. And if not, I do hope you'll have a wonderful day."

He reached for the other coffee from the paper tray, lifted the coffee in mock salute and strolled away, carrying his briefcase.

Rachel watched him for a moment before she forced her attention back to her computer. She had work to do. She wasn't about to let him distract her, and she reached for another book and began her research all over, only it wasn't the same as it had been before because Atticus had seated himself in an overstuffed chair near the window and was pulling a small table close to his side. It aggravated her that he'd chosen a spot in her line of sight and she could see him pull out his laptop and open it up and prepare to work.

He was wearing a blue cashmere sweater and dark trousers, a black leather belt and black leather shoes, and with his hair combed back, he looked annoyingly well put together. And then, just when she thought he couldn't look more sophisticated, he drew a pair of dark framed glasses from his briefcase and slid them on his nose. She'd never met a man so stylish, or sure of himself, and she wondered what his office in Houston was like, and if the lawyers and administration were as stylish as he.

And then she didn't want to think about him anymore, and she lifted one of the boxes of books from the back room and placed it on the counter to block him from her view. It was then, and only then, that she could settle enough to concentrate, and she was finally managing to get some work done when Atticus's deep voice broke the silence.

"Rachel, you're going to need to look into getting internet. Your customers will expect it, and the only way I can get a strong signal on my phone in this building is to step outside."

She slid the box over a couple inches so she could see him. "Feel free to step outside," she said cheerfully. "It's probably the best place for you anyway."

"I won't take that personally."

"Maybe you should."

"I'm thicker skinned than that, darlin'," he said with his easy grin as he collected his paperwork and then put away his laptop.

She felt a prick of guilt when he closed his briefcase, and then her gaze fell on her coffee which she'd sipped when she'd thought he wasn't paying attention. She hadn't been very nice to him, and now he was leaving, and some company was better than no company. "Do you need to use my hotspot?" she offered. "I can share if what you're working on is important."

"That's very generous of you, but I'll just head back to the Graff. I have a conference call at noon so I should get ready for that."

"Thank you for the coffee and scones," she said, as he headed to the door. "It was a nice gesture. I appreciated it."

"My pleasure, Rachel. Hope you have a good first day."

IT WAS A quiet first day, so quiet that Rachel found herself hoping Atticus would drop in again, just so she'd hear a voice. But he didn't return and she stood at the door now, gazing out onto Main Street. Twilight was falling and the tall old-fashioned streetlights were coming on along with the white lights that formed part of the holiday decorations marking the street. At the Mercantile she'd seen flyers about the annual Marietta Stroll, happening on Saturday. She wondered exactly what the stroll was, and where it actually took place. She ought to find out since she'd be here.

But standing inside her store looking out, she wondered if she was making a mistake. She didn't feel as if she belonged and she was missing the structure of her job in Irvine. The lack of routine was making her restless, and the long silent afternoon wore on her. She was happiest being busy, happiest doing what she did best—playing with numbers, calculating taxes and deductions, tackling complicated problems. Entering old books into a spreadsheet wasn't exactly high-level thinking.

But it's only the first day. She left her vigil at the door to walk around the store, going through the travel section to the local history section, where she paused to examine a shelf of books on Butte, and the history of copper mining in Montana. She pulled out a book on the Pleasure Gardens of Butte before sliding it back between other old books, and moved to another shelf featuring early Montana emigrants, cattle drives, and one room schoolhouses. Lesley had collected a lot of interesting books. Did people even know what she had?

Finally at six she returned to the front door and locked it, before turning the sign to *Closed*. She turned off the overhead lights, leaving on the little white lights in the windows, before going upstairs where she turned off all but one, and continued up to the apartment to make a simple pasta dinner.

She ate as she scrolled through the *Wall Street Journal* on her phone, and was studying the Dow Jones when a big bang came from downstairs.

Rachel straightened, and went still, listening intently. What was that?

The loud bang seemed to come from the floor directly below her, but what would make a sound like that?

The front door was locked—she'd made sure of that—and she should be the only one in the building.

Heart thudding, she crept halfway down the attic stairs and crouched on the steps, peeking through the bannister. From where she stood, nothing looked out of order. Night had fallen and the darkness pressed against the windows, a contrast to the sole light she'd left on.

She couldn't see anything out of order, either. Everything looked tidy, and the woodwork glowed, still smelling of the citrus-scented polish she'd used earlier.

She crept down another couple of stairs, and that was when she spotted the big, thick hardback on the ground, lying in front of one of the narrow bookshelves. The book was most definitely not on the floor when she'd been cleaning earlier. So how did it get there? Her glance swept the room, looking to see if anything else appeared out of place, but there was no other noise, or movement. The rest of the second floor was just as she'd left it.

She told herself it was nothing, but she was spooked and

she suddenly didn't want to go back upstairs, either, not on her own. Rachel hurried downstairs, grabbed her coat from the coatrack, unlocked the front door and ran out onto the curb.

Her pulse was racing as she tugged on her coat and zipped it closed. Stepping off the curb and into the street, she warily eyed the windows on the second floor. What made the book fall? And it was just a book, so why was she so scared?

It was silly, really, to be afraid because she didn't believe in ghosts and there was no way Paradise Books was haunted. For one, Lesley would never gift her a building that was haunted, and for another, Rachel was too pragmatic to think all those TV shows about paranormal activity was real.

And then it crossed her mind—what if someone was upstairs?

What if someone had somehow entered the bookstore and was hiding on the second floor, or maybe was now in the attic space? There was access to the store through the door to the alley, as well as the front door, and she'd thought she locked both, but someone could have entered when she wasn't paying attention.

She was still trying to decide what to do when she heard Atticus call her name, and she turned around to see him in his SUV, window rolled down. "What are you doing?" he asked. "Why are you in in the middle of the street?"

"I got spooked, so I ran out. I'm trying to decide what to

do."

"What happened?"

She opened her mouth to try to explain and then realized it would sound foolish. "Don't worry. I'll handle it."

He parked the car in one of the angled spots in front of the store before rolling up his window and stepping out. He was wearing a dark brown sheepskin coat, dark denim jeans, and what looked like a pair of pointed cowboy boots.

"You're all dressed up," she said, not adding that his coat didn't appear to be the practical rancher variety, but the kind worn by Hollywood celebs when they went to the Sundance Film Festival.

"Is that a compliment?" he asked, smiling.

"Just an observation."

His gaze swept over her. "So what are you going to handle?"

She frowned, not sure how to explain without sounding slightly unhinged. "Something weird just happened."

"What?"

"I was up in the attic apartment when I heard a loud bang a floor below." She watched his face, waiting for a change of expression. "When I went down to see what it was, a book was lying in the middle of the second floor, and there's no way a book that big just fell off the shelf on its own. I'd cleaned the room earlier, too, and there were no books left in precarious positions."

"You said you were above?"

"Yes, in the apartment one floor up."

"A heavy vibration might have knocked the book from the shelf."

She made a face. "I'm not that heavy."

"I'm not talking about you. It could have been just about anything—a door slamming, or a truck driving by—"

"The books are crammed in next to each other. How would the vibration of a truck make one book wiggle its way out and slam to the ground?"

"What do you think it was?"

"I don't know. But it was unnerving."

"Do you watch a lot of paranormal shows?"

"*No.*"

"Do you think your building is haunted?" he asked, a little too cheerfully.

"*No.*" She was no longer quite so happy to see him. "But I would like an explanation for the book. It was loud when it fell, and a little bit scary. I'm not easily scared."

"Would you like me to go up and check it out for you?"

Relief swept through her. "Would you?"

"Of course."

"I'll stand in the front door, just in case."

"Just in case the ghost swoops down to steal me?"

She rolled her eyes. "I don't believe in ghosts, and even if ghosts exist, I don't think they steal people. I'm just staying close in case you need backup."

"I appreciate that. Lead the way."

She entered the store, and turned on the lights, skin prickling with awareness as Atticus stood close behind her. She didn't want to feel this strange tingly sensation when she saw him, and she definitely didn't want to feel anything tingly when he spoke to her, but she felt tingly now, and she told herself it was relief, because he was helping her out, not because she was ridiculously attracted to him.

They'd taken two steps in when Rachel heard a faint, scrabbling sound above and froze. "There," she said breathlessly, "did you hear that?"

Atticus stepped around her and entered the store. She watched his face as he listened closely. "I think it's just a mouse," he said after a moment. "Which doesn't surprise me as it's a one hundred-and-twenty-year-old building with two floors of books."

Rachel wasn't reassured. "Can mice knock a big leather-bound book off a shelf?"

"Maybe not a mouse, but a rat could, or a raccoon." He paused, before shrugging. "Or a possum."

"A possum?"

"This is Montana."

"I *know* it's Montana," she retorted, unable to hide her irritation. "You just took me on a scenic drive through Paradise Valley." She glanced to the wooden staircase leading up to the second floor. "But what if it's not a mouse, or a raccoon, or a possum? What if someone's up there? What if someone snuck in when I was working and is hiding upstairs now? Maybe we should call the sheriff."

"We're not going to call the sheriff."

"All right, fine. *I'll* call the sheriff."

"You don't need the sheriff. That's embarrassing."

"Not to me. That's what law enforcement is for."

"*I* will check it out."

She glanced toward the staircase. "What if there's someone hiding up there?"

"Then I'll have to take care of him."

"What if he has a gun?"

"What if I do?"

She blinked, surprised. "*Do you?*"

He shrugged. "The point is, I'm not worried."

"Fine. Be the hero. But if something bad happens to you, I'm calling 911, I'm not coming up."

"Not even partway up the stairs, just to see how bad it is?"

Her lips twitched. He was so exasperating and yet he made her want to laugh, and no one ever made her laugh. She'd been told over and over that she had no sense of humor, that she wasn't fun, that she didn't know how to enjoy anything. "No. You're on your own."

"Some backup you are, Rachel Mills."

ATTICUS WASN'T WORRIED. The scrabbling sound above was definitely a small animal, and there was probably a nest somewhere which needed removing.

"If you need me, yell," Rachel shouted up at him.

He turned around at the top of the stairs and looked down at her, where she was hovering nervously at the bottom of the stairs, blonde hair piled on top of her head, secured with a yellow pencil, the kind he had used in school. "I appreciate that. But if things turn weird up here, save yourself."

She giggled as if she found the idea vastly entertaining. "And if things get weirder and you die up there, I'll rename the store after you."

"Put that on my headstone. Atticus Bowen didn't get the restaurant, but he did get a bookstore."

"Something is better than nothing," she answered, hands on her hips.

He choked on a muffled laugh and glanced around the second floor, looking for the light switch. He found it on the wall, and switched it on. The overhead chandelier cast sparkles of light on the dark wood floor, while everything smelled of old leather, books, and bright fresh lemon. It was an old-fashioned scent and he felt a wash of nostalgia. There weren't many places like Paradise Books left in America. It had once been a much-loved bookstore, but he knew from Troy and Taylor that the bookstore had struggled for the past few years before Lesley had gone to see her sister in Australia.

Atticus had to duck his head as he did a quick but thorough search of the second floor. He found nothing amiss, except for a thick dark green book lying in the middle of the floor. He crossed to pick it up, and turned the hardback with the gilt lettering on the spine, *The Works of Charles Dickens: Christmas Stories*. It was a big book, a very thick book, and still carrying the anthology, he headed up the stairs to inspect the third floor and was pleasantly surprised by the apartment carved from under the steeply sloped ceiling.

Again he checked all areas, from the small living room with a miniature kitchen, to the closets lining the halls, to the tiny bedroom and bathroom at the opposite end. The walls in the living room and kitchen were exposed red brick, while the brick in the bedroom had been covered with a green and silvery-blue botanical paper. The staircase formed a natural divider between the two spaces and a thick door could be shut at the bottom of the stairs, making the apartment secure.

After a search through the final closet, Atticus was confident there was no one lurking anywhere upstairs, and he headed back down to give Rachel the news that there was nothing for her to be afraid of. "Whatever it was that knocked the book off the shelf is gone, but I did bring the book down. It looks like it wants to be read." He set the book on the counter and looked at her. "Or maybe bought by someone who loves a good Dickens Christmas story."

She opened the book and flipped to the copyright date, 1882. The book was square and tight and clean. It was in remarkable shape really. Rachel glanced up at Atticus. "Maybe it wants to be part of my Christmas display."

Atticus didn't contradict her, but she sensed from his pursed lips he wanted to. "What?" she said suspiciously.

His broad shoulders lifted and fell. "I didn't say anything."

"Exactly. You always have something to say."

"You're just finding your footing. It's not my place—"

"You don't like my window displays," she interrupted. "Do you?"

"You're new at this. You're learning."

"I actually like you better when you're being blunt. Please just spit it out."

"I think you need to add some height to your display. You haven't really utilized all that space. Your windows still appear empty."

She shot him a narrowed glance before marching outside to have a look for herself. If she stood very close to the window she could see the flowers and three books, but if she stepped back, to the corner, or even further away, all she saw was empty space.

He was right, she thought, biting her bottom lip. It wasn't a very dynamic display. "It could use some help," she said evenly, trying to keep the discouragement from her voice. She wasn't the most artistic person out there, nor apparently, did she have a crafty bone in her body, which was frustrating because she'd tried hard to make the new display appealing.

"You need something vertical, even a ladder would help," he said after a moment. "The windows are really tall, and your display right now is all at the bottom so people can't really see anything until they're standing quite close to the glass."

"So put the poinsettias on a ladder?"

"I'd put books on the ladder, and to be honest, I'm not sure the poinsettias are helping you out very much."

Rachel frowned. "You don't like poinsettias?"

"I don't dislike them, but I don't think they're interesting enough to make people want to look at your windows."

Rachel's confidence just continued to fall. "This isn't my strength."

"I understand, and I wasn't going to say something because I don't want to be critical. I'd like to be your friend—"

"Huh."

"At the same time, you're competing with other stores. Your windows should make people want to look, not look away."

Ouch. "It's that bad?"

"Let's go for a walk. See what everyone else is doing." He hesitated. "Or have you already done that?"

"I still haven't really explored Marietta," she admitted. "I've been to the Graff to meet you, Grey's Saloon for dinner my first night here, and then I walked to the Mercantile this morning, but I was so focused on getting what I needed I didn't really look around."

"Unless you're dying to get back upstairs—"

"I'm not."

"Then how about we take a walk and then on the way back we hit Main Street Diner for dessert since you haven't been there yet, and they're famous for their breakfasts and homemade cakes and pies."

"Homemade cakes and pies? You're right. I can't miss that."

AFTER CROSSING THE street the first shop on the corner was Risa's Flowers and one of the corner windows featured a giant wreath, while the other window, the one facing Main Street, featured a dozen different pedestals, each topped by a different topiary ball covered in red or green ornaments. Smaller topiary trees and plants were tucked around the base of the white and glass pedestals. At the very top of the window hung three oversized red ball lights, playing off the ornament theme in the window.

Rachel cocked her head and studied the display that filled the entire window. The florist had only made use of three colors, and it wasn't a busy display, but she found it fascinating anyway. "I like this," she said after a moment. "But I'm not sure why."

"It's a statement display," Atticus said. "It's modern and sculptural and yet it has a big impact because those smooth satin ball ornaments are a great contrast to the soft leafy topiaries."

"Maybe that's what I like," she answered. "That it's more modern and not fussy. I'm not a fan of fussy anything."

He smiled. "I look forward to hearing what you have to say about the next shop, which is undoubtedly Marietta's most popular business."

They took a dozen steps and ended up in front of Copper Mountain Chocolates. A giant chocolate Santa guard above red and gold boxes with lavish ribbon. A tiered tray of salted caramels anchored one corner of the window, while smaller chocolate Santas in cellophane and red ribbon filled a red painted box at the other end. And in between the caramels and gold and red boxes were chocolate houses, dusted with powdered sugar to resemble sparkling snow. Rachel's mouth watered. "I would go in here," she said.

"You haven't been in yet?"

She shook her head. "The Copper Mountain Chocolate's hot cocoa at Bramble House, but I haven't been able to come down and pop in when the store is open."

"Promise me tomorrow you'll walk down here and introduce yourself. I'm not sure if Sage will be working, but she has a really good staff and Sage is beloved by everyone in Marietta."

"How do you know so much about her?"

"She's Troy Sheenan's half sister."

"They grew up together?"

"No." He turned away from the window, and took her arm, steering her forward. "And that's not a story for me to tell, but I'm sure if you got to know the Carrigans or Sheenans, they'd tell you themselves."

They crossed one more street and then came to a shop where the window was filled with a gingerbread town and gingerbread people and even a gingerbread courthouse capped with a glass dome, and then Rachel clapped. "This is Marietta," she said. "This is Main Street—oh, look! There's Grey's Saloon and that's my bookstore, and there, over behind the train tack, that must be the Graff Hotel."

"I see the courthouse," Atticus said. "And I think that must be the library over there."

"We're just missing Bramble House," Rachel answered, as they walked on to the next store Atticus wanted her to see.

They passed the travel agency and then an insurance agency before stopping in front of a window filled with delicate birch trees and pine trees and glittering snow. It was essentially a winter wonderland, with trees and birds, and a frozen pond.

Rachel took a step closer, trying to see everything. "This is incredible," she murmured. "I could never, not in a million years, do something like this. It's magical."

"Sadie Douglas is pretty talented."

"You know her?"

"I was introduced to her and her husband, Rory, at the Sheenans summer party last July. Troy's twin brother Trey is married to McKenna Douglas, and McKenna is the sister of Rory Douglas—" He broke off as he noticed her bewildered expression. "It sounds more complicated than it is. The Sheenans and Douglases were ranchers and neighbors in Paradise Valley, and Sadie married the eldest Douglas, which made the community happy because Rory needed a miracle and by all accounts married an angel."

"I spent my whole life in Irvine and know almost no one. You've been here—how many times—and seem to know everyone."

"It's a tight-knit community. I like it here."

"How many times have you visited?"

"A dozen times? Maybe more? I try to come as often as I can."

"Would you ever live here?"

"I've thought about it. If the restaurant opens here, it might become my new home base."

She eyed him a long moment before turning back to the window, and reading the sign above the shop. *The Montana Rose*. "What is her shop? I can't tell what she's selling," Rachel said.

"Sadie's an interior designer with a wonderful selection of vintage Christmas ornaments and decorations, along with custom furniture."

"Why not put those in the window?"

"She does something different with her window every year. Last year she had her vintage trees. This year it's a snowy meadow."

"But she's not actually selling her products in the window."

"I think the point is to get you to stop and look. If the store was open, would you go inside?"

"Probably." She sighed heavily, and crossed her arms over her chest. "But let's be honest, everything I've seen tonight is way out of my league. Even on my best day, I'd never be able to do any of these things."

"I don't think anyone would expect you to do something really elaborate," he answered. "But you could certainly do more with what you have."

She pictured the bookstore, and tried to imagine what she could do with what she already had. What if she took one of the reading chairs from the store and put it in the window next to a table stacked with books? Maybe add a lamp and a folded blanket, making it look like a cozy reading corner. And then she groaned inwardly because it sounded like a thrift shop window display now. "What am I doing here? This is crazy."

"Come on, chin up. Don't let the window stuff get to you. It's really not that big of a deal."

"It obviously is, or we wouldn't be out here." She hunched her shoulders and shook her head. "I'm sorry. I'm just really frustrated."

"Understandable. You're out of your comfort zone."

"Yes. Fashion, style, design… those are not my areas of

expertise. I'm a math geek without a lick of creativity. I was excited about my windows and now I'm just embarrassed. They were awful—"

"Stop. No more. Your teeth are chattering and I can't just let you stand here and freeze," he said, linking his arm with hers. "I promised you dessert and that's what we're going to do."

CHAPTER FIVE

THE DINER WAS wonderfully warm after the chilly night, and relatively empty giving them their pick of booths. Atticus suggested a table along the front windows, their dark red booth just beneath a pair of painted angels singing "Hark the Herald" on the glass.

Rachel sat down and peeled off the mittens she always kept stashed in her coat pockets. "It feels good in here. I can't get over the cold. It's *winter*."

"Most of the country has a real winter. We're the exception," he answered, placing his coat on the bench next to him.

"Do you like Houston?" she asked.

"Yes," he answered, pointing out the pies and cakes of the day, written on the chalkboard. "See what I mean about options?"

She read the listings—so many delicious desserts—but they had her favorite, an old-fashioned chocolate layer cake with chocolate frosting, and Rachel didn't need to look anymore. "What do you like about Houston?" she asked, determined to get him to talk since he seemed to ask a lot of questions rather than share much about himself.

"It's home."

She arched a brow. "That's it?"

"There is a lot to like. The culture, the art, food. It's pretty diverse, and it's an interesting place to do what I do since there is no formal zoning code. It's why the urban sprawl can appear so confusing to the outsider."

"I've never been," she confessed. "And I've heard it's a big city, where you drive and drive, and drive."

"It's smaller than Los Angeles."

That wasn't saying much, she thought. "Where's your office?"

"Downtown Houston."

"Is it your own business?"

"Yes."

"You give very short answers."

He cracked a smile. "I'm a former trial attorney. I hate revealing anything."

"In case it gets used against you?"

"Absolutely."

"You're not a trial attorney anymore?" she asked.

"I switched to real estate law."

"Why?"

"Is this a deposition?"

"You really hate answering questions."

Creases fanned from his eyes. "You picked up on that, did you?"

She shook her head. "You're impossible."

"That's not the first time I've heard that."

They paused to place their order and when the waitress walked away, Rachel said, "It must be nice having control of your own schedule."

"It's one of the better perks about my work now."

"Do you miss anything about being a litigator?"

He hesitated so long she wasn't sure he would answer. "I felt like I was doing something good," he said at length. "I felt like I had a purpose."

"You don't anymore?"

"It's a different kind of good, and a different kind of purpose. Maybe because the stakes are different."

She wanted to reply to this, but the waitress returned with their cups of coffee—regular for Atticus, and decaf for her—and after the waitress left, it somehow didn't seem right to pursue the subject. Or maybe Atticus's hard, shuttered expression made her reluctant to push.

Rachel added milk to her coffee and gave it a slow, thoughtful stir. "Work is a strange thing," she said after a moment. "It's certainly consuming. This is my first real break in years. I've taken a day here and there, but never two full weeks off at one time."

"Your company discourages staff from taking vacation time?"

"No. I just always feel like I have too much to do to take time off. I have weeks and weeks coming to me—and I was going to lose three of those at the end of this year if I didn't take them—which is partly why I'm here now rather than January or February."

"I'm glad it wasn't hard for you to take two weeks at one time."

She grimaced. "Oh, they didn't like it. In fact, at first I was told it couldn't happen, that it wasn't convenient, but when I threatened to quit they backed down. So here I am."

"Will you face a backlash when you return?"

She thought of work and wasn't sure if she should laugh or cry. It had been such a roller coaster the past few years, and she still felt so deflated after being passed over for the last promotion. "I would have worried two months ago. I'm not as concerned anymore."

He gave her a penetrating look. "Did something happen?"

"It's just an annoying thing. Not worth talking about." She sipped her coffee, enjoying its warmth. "I will say, though, that I miss my work routine. I'm struggling a bit without it. This afternoon seemed to last forever. I would have given almost anything to be at my desk, in my office, pouring over real numbers instead of deciding whether or not a hundred-year-old book is worth keeping."

"I would think the monetary value would be the indication."

"So would I, but it's not quite so cut and dried. Some of the books have exquisite illustrations. Others have lovely gilt edges and delicate pages—" She broke off and gave her head a shake. "Accounting is black and white. The book business isn't."

"Can you make it more black and white?"

"I'm trying. It'd be easier if it was."

"Aren't there online bookstore that will tell you whether or not your book is important?"

"Yes, there are, and I'm using those, but sometimes the books have secrets that don't increase the value."

"What do you mean by secrets?"

"Maybe there's a better word, but as I've been going through the boxes of books I've found books with sweet inscriptions, books with slips of paper inside, where someone saved a dance card, or a ticket stub, or a shopping list. In one book I even found a republican ticket with a list of candidates from 1881."

"That must be fascinating."

"It is, but it complicates the book business. What do you do with the dance card, and the ticket stub, and the republican ticket?"

"Leave it inside the book?"

"That's what I've done, but some of those books aren't valuable, so theoretically they shouldn't be kept."

"But if you see value in them, can't you keep them?"

"I would if there was a place to put them. Lesley's store shelves are crammed full. I can't see keeping a storage room filled with boxes."

The waitress returned with her cake and his slice of banana cream pie.

"Why not reach out to Lesley and ask her?"

Rachel slowly lowered her fork. "Ask her what?"

"Ask her whatever you don't know. Ask whatever you want to know. Ask to see her profit and loss statement going back five years—"

"I couldn't do that."

"Why not? You look at everyone else's financials."

"That's different. I'm their accountant."

"But wouldn't it be nice to see her operating numbers?"

Absolutely, Rachel thought. It would make a huge difference, but she also understood why Lesley might not want her to see them—if Lesley was operating in the red, she might be afraid the debt would scare Rachel away. "I've seen some of her taxes from three years ago. There wasn't a lot of income."

"What about monthly? Which months were her best months? Which months were the leanest?"

"Atticus, I've only met her a couple times in my life, the last time at my mother's funeral. If she walked in here now, I don't think I'd even recognize her."

"I think you would. I've never met her but what I've heard she's short with curly gray hair and a big smile. Think Angela Lansbury."

"Except that Angela Lansbury is five eight, not five one."

"How do you know Angela Lansbury's height?"

"My grandmother Gerber—that was my mom's maiden

name—was a huge fan of *Murder She Wrote* and whenever I'd stay over at her house, we'd watch it, so in fifth grade I ended up doing a book report on her character, Jessica Fletcher, and the fictional town of Cabot Cove, and I read that Angela was five eight."

"You've remembered that detail all these years?"

"I have a gift for numbers."

"Yes, you do."

They fell silent for several minutes as they ate, and then Atticus said, "You do know it's okay to ask for help, don't you? No one expects anyone to be able to do everything perfectly."

Rachel's cheeks heated. She felt vaguely nauseous and suddenly didn't feel much like eating anymore. "Where did that little gem come from?"

"I'm not criticizing you," he said almost gently.

She drank her coffee because she didn't know what to say or do. She wasn't good at asking for help, and it didn't help that she was a perfectionist. She expected herself to execute things flawlessly. For that matter, learning new things wasn't one of her strengths, and it had been a struggle the past few days trying to figure out the store. "I am doing my best, but I am truly out of my element. I specialize in numbers and am awash in words and I honestly don't know why Lesley gave me, of all people, the store. I'm the last person who should be in charge of something like this."

"Why don't you ask her that?"

"Because it would feel like defeat, and I'm not a defeatest."

"But you're also not a machine. You have questions, you have feelings—"

"Ugh. Please don't say that ever again."

He threw his head back and laughed. "You don't like feelings?"

"I avoid them whenever possible."

"You make me smile," he said.

"I'm not trying to."

His smile just widened and the smile was so gorgeous and sexy it made her heart do a silly flip. "If I can help you sometime, will you let me?" he asked.

"You've already helped me a lot. You took me for that lovely drive. You made sure there was nothing scary lurking in my building. You even showed me what good window displays looked like."

"You're not mad about that?"

"No, I appreciate it. I value the truth."

"So do I," he said quietly, his blue gaze meeting hers and holding, the expression in his eyes so warm it put fresh butterflies in her middle.

After a moment, she dropped her gaze and fidgeted in her seat. "Here's a truth," she said lowly, "if I called Lesley, I wouldn't ask about the store."

"No?"

"No." She kept her gaze locked on her plate. "I'd ask

about my mom."

She waited for him to say something but he didn't, and she hated all the yawning silence, a silence that made her feel too much and God help her, she wasn't good with emotions. Feelings. Love, loss, pain. There had been so much loss and pain when her mother was sick, and even more loss and pain after she was gone.

"I would hope Lesley could tell me things I've forgotten," she added, digging the prongs of her fork into the thick icing and peeling it from the layers.

"I don't remember enough about my mom," she said after another beat. "When I'm at the office, buried in work, I can block out everything but the work. But here, I've so much time on my hands and I find myself thinking about things the way they were before Mom died, and I just come up... blank. My entire past has become something of a blur."

"What happened to your mom?"

"Cancer. She was diagnosed at the end of my freshman year, and was gone by October of my senior year. High school is fuzzy. My senior year is fuzzy—I literally remember nothing after the funeral. Even before she was sick is now foggy. Why can't I remember more?"

"You were young and something devastating happened. Sounds like your brain tried to protect you."

"I don't blame my brain. I blame me. After she died, I didn't want to think about her. Hospice sucked. I didn't want to remember her the way she was at the end. It was awful. She was so skinny—all bones and bruises—and it was hard to look at her. I didn't even want to hug her because I was afraid it'd hurt her, and maybe she'd break—" She exhaled hard, and fought to keep her voice even. "I wished I hugged her so much more. I regret being afraid—"

"You were a teenager, Rachel."

"Doesn't matter," she retorted fiercely. "Once people are gone, they don't come back." She reached up and brushed fingertips beneath her eyes, not about to let tears form or fall. "I worked so hard to block out the bad memories that now I can't remember anything."

"Other than grandparents, I've never lost anyone close to me," Atticus said after a moment. "So I can't even imagine what you've been through. I'm just sorry you had to experience so much loss so young."

Rachel grimaced. "I don't even know why I'm telling you this. I never talk about this."

"Maybe I'm a good listener?"

"Or maybe you want that bookstore really badly."

"What does that mean?" he demanded, sitting taller, his deep voice sharpening.

She was feeling prickly and out of sorts and she shrugged impatiently. "You're 'befriending' me," she answered bluntly, doing air quotes around the word befriending, "to increase your odds for ending up with the store."

He now looked as annoyed as she felt. "I don't need to

befriend you to get the store. I'm hanging out with you because I like you." He must have seen her expression because he added, "Is that really so shocking?"

Her prickly defensiveness just increased. "I'm on the nerdy side, and I know it."

"Nerds can be cool."

"You think so?"

"Of course. I've been a nerd my whole life, and I love my life. It's interesting and I'm myself and I wouldn't have it any other way."

"Nobody is going to meet you and think you're a nerd."

"Nobody is going to meet you and think you're a nerd, either. You're beautiful—"

"Oh, come on."

"Don't you look in the mirror?"

"I try to avoid it."

"Why?"

"I just don't—" She broke off, shoulders twisting. "Find my appearance all that interesting. There are other things I'd rather focus on."

"Like numbers?"

She smiled ruefully. "Well, yes."

"Men are attracted to you, Rachel. You must know that."

"I don't really pay attention."

"Maybe that's the problem. Maybe you should pay more attention to the world around you."

"Ugh. Now you sound like my dad. He's begun talking

about trying to set me up with one of his former grad students." She shuddered. "I can't think of anything worse."

"Why?"

Rachel flashed back to Eric and the demise of their relationship. He wanted so much more from her, and he couldn't understand why—at her age—she wasn't ready to settle down. "My last relationship ended in May when I chose to focus on my career and not on 'us.'" She stabbed the cake, cutting a big bite. "He was a nice guy, and probably a really good catch. My father certainly liked him—they'd talk economics for hours—but I wasn't ready to get engaged, and settle down."

"So he broke it off?"

"No, I did. I didn't think it was fair to string him along."

"Don't feel guilty. He wasn't the right guy."

"How do you know?" she asked, before popping the big bite into her mouth. Soft, moist cake with thick creamy, not too sweet, icing. For a second she felt almost human again.

"Because you wouldn't let the right guy go," Atticus added. "You'd fight for him."

She lifted a brow, challenging him. Atticus was impossibly confident but she secretly found it quite appealing.

Atticus shrugged. "You fight for everything else, why wouldn't you fight for your true love?"

She sipped coffee to wash the cake down. "Maybe because I don't believe in true love. I think there is compatibility and respect and all of that, but I think the whole falling in love, can't live without you stuff is a lot of commercial nonsense."

Atticus just grinned and polished off his pie.

She leaned forward, and nearly pulled his plate away from him. "Why are you looking smug?"

"Because when you fall, sweet girl, you're going to fall so hard."

"Not going to happen."

He just gave her another knowing smile. "We'll see."

HE'D WANTED TO kiss her at the diner, and he wanted to hold her hand as they crossed the street, heading back to the bookstore, but he couldn't do either.

He liked her a lot, and she was already conflicted about the store, and him, and he didn't want to add more pressure. There was a lot going on in her life right now and she needed someone to make things easier for her, not harder.

They reached her corner and they stood now before Paradise Books's front door. "Do you want me to see you up to the apartment?" he asked. "Make sure it's all good?"

"You did that earlier. I'm sure the mouse or rat or whatever it was has gone to sleep. Besides, if you walked me up, I'd still have to come down to lock the door behind you, so I'm better off just saying goodbye here."

"I don't think you have anything to be afraid of."

"I refuse to be afraid."

If she was his, he'd kiss her now. If she was his, he'd kiss her all the time. "Smart girl."

She gave him a crooked smile before unlocking the door and stepping inside. "Thank you for the company, and the advice, and the investigative work earlier."

He smiled wryly. "My pleasure."

"Good night, Atticus."

"Good night, Rachel."

He waited for the dead bolt to lock, and the lights to come on and then turn off, as she moved through the various floors. He waited until he saw light shine from the window at the very top before returning to his car.

Tonight he'd met a prospective client out on the client's property in Paradise Valley before driving into town to meet Cormac Sheenan at Gray's Saloon to discuss a new project Cormac had in mind. It didn't take very long to drive the three blocks to the Graff, passing the Depot and crossing the railroad tracks. He was just entering the hotel when he spotted Troy Sheenan on his way out.

"Are you just now wrapping up that meeting with Cormac?" Troy asked.

"No, that ended a couple hours ago. I've been with Rachel. Showed her around and then grabbed a bite at the diner."

"You're spending a lot of time with her."

"Is that a problem?"

"Just curious about your motives."

Atticus stiffened, not liking the implication. "She's an outsider here. She doesn't know many people. We're both outsiders—"

"Who both just happen to be interested in the same thing."

"Exactly." Atticus was silent a moment as he regarded his long-time friend and business associate. "You're not worried my restaurant is going to cut into your business at the Graff, are you? Right now you're the top dog here for fine dining."

Troy shrugged dismissively. "Marietta can handle the competition, and a Galveston Steak House could even help fill the Graff's rooms, but there are a lot of other locations in Marietta that would work for your restaurant. It doesn't have to be the bookstore."

"But the bookstore is exactly what I want. It has the ideal location on Main Street, positioned on the corner. The brick interior and exterior are in excellent shape. The two stories are perfect for the dining room, and then it has that deep back mechanical room which would make an ideal kitchen, as well as a basement which would give us space for an elevator, and proper bathrooms, allowing us to bring the building to code in terms of accessibility."

"You could probably fight that one, based on the building's age and historical value."

"I wouldn't, though. I might be cutthroat with my deals, but once a building is mine, I take care of it, and you know I'm an advocate for accessibility. Fortunately, my architect and design team have tackled that issue in other buildings I've acquired so I'm not worried about it."

"But the building in question is not available."

"It will be."

Troy arched a brow.

"Rachel is a realist, not a romantic. She's aware that bookstores, particularly stores that rely on used books, don't generate enough revenue to pay for the overhead. She's lucky that there isn't a mortgage, but she will still have to pay utilities and taxes, and there isn't going to be a lot left over. Just keeping that place warm in winter will drain her finances. She's going to sell to me, one way or another. It's just a question of when."

"Unless she's willing to do something different with the bookstore." Troy smiled faintly. "Maybe she'll open her own restaurant."

"I don't see that happening."

"Why not?"

"She's already out of her element."

"And what if she sold to someone?"

"Someone like Taylor?" Atticus retorted, remembering the rather tense conversation following dinner at the Sheenans earlier in the week.

"Taylor is committed to Marietta's library. She's not looking to take on the bookstore, but she believes in the store and she'd hate to think you're undermining Rachel in any way."

Atticus suppressed his frustration. "I care about Rachel—"

"You don't have to sell me."

"Troy, I *like* her, and I'm not going to do anything that would hurt her." He nodded to Troy and said good night and as he rode the elevator to the suite on the fourth floor, his words echoed in his head.

He really did care for her, and the last thing he wanted to do was hurt her, or keep her from succeeding with the bookstore. While he still wanted the building, he also wanted her happiness. Was there a way they could both get what they wanted?

Atticus was no longer so sure.

IT WAS A magnificent sunrise, the sky behind the mountains turning pink and then glowing persimmon and gold.

She'd had good dreams, dreams that had left her waking up smiling. If only she remembered them. But at least she'd slept well, and there had been no more bumps in the night, and now she sat on the foot of her bed gazing out the oval window, with its view of majestic Copper Mountain, covered in white.

The little apartment this morning was chilly, but the view more than made up for the cold. She drew the quilt draped over her shoulders closer, huddling into the warmth with her mug of coffee clutched between her hands and as she sat there watching the sun slowly rise up behind the mountains, she felt a bubble of lightness within her, and the bubble seemed to get bigger, much like the sun appearing in the sky.

The lightness felt almost like excitement, or maybe happiness. She didn't know what would happen today but she had a feeling it would be interesting, if she could let new things be interesting instead of frustrating or intimidating.

Atticus was right. She did put a lot of pressure on herself. Sometimes it was too much pressure. Maybe just for now she could give herself permission to enjoy change, and a break from the familiar, and not have to be perfect. Maybe she could enjoy a break from her routine, and not feel insecure because she was learning something new.

If she was this rigid and inflexible at thirty, imagine being fifty? Seventy? My goodness, the future looked bleak at the rate she was going. So, now, while she was on her vacation, she needed to relax, and embrace Marietta and Montana.

She thought of her walk around Marietta last night with Atticus looking at window displays, and then dessert at the diner after, and she felt a pang just remembering how he'd made her feel…

She'd dated Eric for a year and he'd never made her feel tingly or breathless. She'd never felt a tender pang, or gotten butterflies when he looked at her.

Atticus made her feel all that… and more.

She was entering uncharted territory. Dangerous territory.

It crossed her mind that she was beginning to care for him a little too much, and she ought to know better. She needed to guard her heart better, protect her emotions, be realistic, be proactive. In short, be smart, because that was what had gotten her this far in life.

Ready to get her day going, Rachel headed to the bathroom for a quick shower before dressing in jeans, a T-shirt, and a thick sweater for warmth. Feet in sturdy boots, she slipped her phone into her back pocket, and went to the kitchen to make oatmeal. With her bowl of oatmeal, Rachel headed downstairs, and opened the shutters one by one, and turned on the lights.

Pale gold sunlight flooded the bookstore. Long rays of golden light streaked the hardwood floor. Air caught in her throat, and for a moment she felt an almost intolerable ache. She'd become so good at not feeling, that when she did, emotion made her miserable. But the bookstore was beautiful and the blue sky was beautiful, as were the snowcapped mountains just outside of town. It was as if Marietta had become magical and she didn't know what to do with all the sensations and emotions.

Work, maybe. Finish her oatmeal and concentrate.

Rachel ended up behind the counter at the cash register, and sighed as she looked at the enormous vintage register. She pressed a few buttons, drew the lever on the side, and the bottom drawer came out. How on earth did Lesley use this for her business? The brass register was beautiful but not at all practical.

To be fair, everything about this store fell into that category.

Computer open, she tackled another box of books from the storage room. She opened the top book, *The Flying Boys to the Rescue*, and paused on the inscription.

1921
A Merry Christmas
To Victor
From Grandpa
and Aunt Cecilia

Rachel dutifully typed the info about the novel into the search engine. The book was listed at ten dollars on several sites. It wasn't a valuable book, but it was part of a set. She looked through the box. There were no more books in the set in the box.

She couldn't really afford to keep the book. Where would she put it? There were other copies available online. Swallowing hard, Rachel set *The Flying Boys to the Rescue* in the discard pile, an uncomfortable lump in her throat, as her eyes burned, dry and gritty.

She shouldn't feel sad that she couldn't keep the book. It wasn't feasible to keep every book from the back room, but it felt as if she'd inherited not a store, but a collection of lives and loves, of memories and dreams. She felt responsible for a past that only lived on in these old books with their faded fabric cloth, and tattered paper covers.

She'd spent the past several days trying to determine a book's value by looking up the age and condition in online databases, but the database didn't truly convey a book's value.

The database didn't take into account the love behind the gift of a book. The database didn't care.

Somehow she did, though, and the emotions baffled her.

She didn't focus on emotion, and she certainly didn't want to care for these books. There were so many, and they were just sitting here, collecting dust. No one wanted them anymore. No one seemed to need them.

Determined to be ruthless, she grabbed a pale green book from the bottom of the box. *Altemus' Young People's History of the United States*, and flipped open the cover.

To Geo A Potter
September 08, 1905
From Pop
Happy Birthday

No.

No.

She wasn't going to do this anymore. She wasn't going to care. The books could go. The books could all go. She was too sensible to become caught up in this impossible task. There was no reason to fall apart over a collection of old books.

The books only mattered if someone was willing to pay for them. They would only be saved if they had measurable financial value. That was it. There was no room for sentimental decisions. No room for wistful feelings. The past was the past, and the only way to survive was to be realistic about the future.

The bell on the front door tinkled as the door swung open. Zane walked in carrying a large cardboard box. He placed the books on the counter where Rachel had been working. She lifted an eyebrow. "More books?"

"Lesley's personal Christmas collection. They're from her house. I used to bring them over for her every year to display, and figured you might want to use them in your windows, too."

He didn't like her windows, either. "I'm not done with my windows," she said. "I have a plan."

"Well, maybe these will help. They're mostly children's books. Classics as well as contemporaries. She'd display in the windows, and read from them during story hour."

Rachel's spirits sank. She couldn't even imagine reading out loud to a bunch of restless children. "Let's see this collection," she said, forcing a cheerful note into her voice.

He opened the box and lifted out stacks of books, and yes, they were nearly all children's books, mostly picture books along with some illustrated classics, ranging from *'Twas the Night Before Christmas*, to books from her childhood like *A Charlie Brown Christmas*, *Santa Mouse*, and *Frosty the Snowman*, and then there were newer books she'd never heard of, including *A Christmas Card for Mr. McFizz* and *Mouse's Christmas Gift* that had her leafing through the pages right away.

"These will be really fun to display," Rachel said.

"Lesley has more at her house for other holidays. I should ask her if she wants to hang on to them," Zane said, lifting a picture book called *Mortimer's Christmas Manager* and opening the cover. "My kids love this one. I should get them a copy."

"Why do they like it?" she asked, curious.

"They love the stories with mice and animals," he said, flipping through the pages quickly, "and this one has exceptional illustrations. See?" He turned the book around for her to see. "The illustrations are big and bright, which appeals to children, plus it has a Christmas message. My wife's a speech therapist and she likes to find things for the kids that are entertaining, but also educational."

"Thus, the popularity of children's books," Rachel said.

"Parents will spend money on their kids that they won't spend on themselves."

"I should be carrying a lot more children's books," Rachel said thoughtfully. "Lesley used to have a huge children's business, but over time she stopped ordering in as much stock, which is a shame because at one point she was going to move the children's section from upstairs where it's tucked behind the adult fiction into a dedicated children's room down here in that big back room."

"That would actually be a good place for it. There's a lot of space."

"And it's close to the only bathroom."

Rachel reached for *Mouse's Christmas Gift* and studied the cover which featured a mouse dressed in a green vest lighting a candle in a frost-covered window. "Why didn't she?"

"That's a good question." Zane restacked all the picture books except for the one in front of her. "But if this was my store, I'd create that dedicated children's room and fill it with children's books, have regular story time, and let everyone know." He tipped the brim of his cowboy hat. "If you need anything, let me know."

"Thank you," she said. "You've been a big help." And he had, she thought, as the door closed behind him because *Mouse's Christmas Gift* had just given her an idea.

What if she frosted part of her windows? Why not hire someone to come and paint sparkly snowflakes on the corners of her two big windows, filling some of the vast space, creating a scene in the middle? She could then use that middle space to highlight Lesley's children's books. She needed a tower, or some big boxes, something to give height, but it was certainly doable.

She paged through *Mouse's Christmas Gift*, reading the short, simple story and found herself blinking back tears as she reached the end. It was not a complicated story but it was beautiful, and moving. Maybe she could display the book next to a Nativity set as the Nativity figured prominently in the story.

Where could she find an inexpensive one? Would that store on Main Street specializing in shabby chic items carry something like that? She'd have to find out first chance she got.

Chapter Six

The door chimed again and Rachel glanced up from her computer hoping to greet her very first customer. It was Atticus. He'd returned.

Like yesterday, he entered the store with his briefcase and cup of coffee. He walked to the chair that he had claimed as his own the day before and removed his coat. Just like yesterday, he pulled the side table close and set up his laptop next to his coffee and pulled out fat folders from the briefcase, the folders filled with paper. He got out a pen, and his phone, and settled down to work.

Yesterday she'd been exasperated.

Today she was amused.

She didn't know why he kept showing up and yet she was secretly glad, grateful for the company. He was surprisingly good company.

She reached for yet another book from the box, this one a thick book with a crumbling red leather binding. *Greek Mythology*, the title read. As she opened the book the front cover fell away from the spine, and loose pages fell out. Not good. She probably needed to dispose of this one, too, and it didn't make her feel terribly bad because there was no one's name inside.

"You know what you need?" Atticus asked, his deep voice breaking the quiet.

"Besides good Wi-Fi?" she said, looking over at him.

He slid on his dark-framed glasses. "An espresso machine."

"Oh, Atticus, no."

"If you had the ability to make espressos, business would skyrocket. I guarantee."

"I have *no* desire to be a barista. Besides, I don't think Java Café would appreciate the competition."

"They can handle it. They're busy, too busy, and too noisy to be able to focus. This is much better here."

She fought a laugh. She couldn't reward him. It would be so wrong because it would just encourage him and he was already a whole lot of lot. "You mean, because no one is here?"

"It is very peaceful," he agreed.

"I do get customers."

"Really?"

"Zane had just dropped by. And you're here again today."

"Did Zane buy anything?"

"You haven't yet."

"Well, you know what I want to buy."

"Do you torture everyone?"

"Lately, it's just been you."

"Lucky me," she said, but she was smiling.

"If you don't want to have to sell to me, I recommend expanding your offerings. You'd get far more foot traffic with an espresso machine."

"So far, no one has asked for a mocha."

"Because you don't sell them," he said patiently. "But if you did, you'd have a steady stream of traffic all day long. The young moms and retirees in the morning, the business crowd at lunch, and students in the afternoon."

"You're describing a coffeehouse, not a bookstore."

"They are thriving businesses, Rachel."

"This will be a thriving business one day, too."

"You have two floors of glorious books, and nothing anyone actually wants to buy." He gestured to the stack of Christmas books still on the counter. "The books people might want to buy are for display purposes only. You can't approach this bookselling thing for the traditional approach. You have to think out of the box."

"I'm trying."

"Good, because you won't like Paradise Books sapping you dry."

"Just last night you were telling me to be positive."

"Yes, be positive, but also realistic. I don't want to see you take a significant loss on this place. I don't think you do, either."

"Every time I think I just might like you, you say or do

something to spoil my good will."

Atticus gave her another of his lethal smiles. "I do love your candor."

"And I would love your help. How long do you intend to be here today?" she asked.

"An hour or two. Why?"

"I have an errand I need to run. Do you mind watching the store for me?"

"You trust me that much?"

He was gorgeous and insufferable, and surprisingly addictive. "Yes." She reached for her purse. "I'll just be down the street so if you need me, call or text."

"I don't have your number."

She scribbled it down on the notepad on the counter. "It's here," she said. "In case of an emergency." And then she grabbed her coat and was off.

Rachel snuggled into her coat as she briskly walked north on Main Street, heading for Sadie's Montana Rose store. If Sadie specialized in vintage Christmas items, surely she'd have a Nativity set.

Sadie wasn't working though, and the shop's sales assistant suggested that Rachel try *Brandel's Baubles, Treasures and Fine Art*, a newer Marietta business that had been opened last April on the southwest corner of Fourth and Main. The owner, Dinah Brandel, was from New Orleans and had some really interesting things. Apparently, Sadie Douglas was a fan of the store and liked to shop there herself.

Rachel thanked the sales assistant and continued down Main. *Brandel's Baubles* was on the first floor of a two-story building, with a large display front window. Pushing open the heavy glass door, she peeked in. Glass display cabinets glittered with jewelry, art, and delicate porcelain figurines.

A woman called out a warm greeting, and from her rich, Southern accent, Rachel suspected this was Dinah Brandel herself. Rachel explained what she was looking for and Dinah shook her head. "I had one, and it sold just this weekend. I can try to find you one. Is there something in particular you're looking for?"

"No. I was just thinking I'd do a display with it. I have the bookstore two blocks down on the corner. Paradise Books."

"It's been closed since I moved here."

"Well, it's open now. If anyone is looking for a hard to find book, send them my way as it seems to be all we carry." Rachel smiled wryly, trying not to feel frustrated.

She would never get people into the store with used books. She needed new ones, like Lesley's pretty children's picture books, that she could actually sell.

"Anything else I can do to help your display?" Dinah asked.

"I don't know. I have all these cute Christmas books featuring mice, and I was trying to think of something fun to do with them."

Dinah's expression brightened. "How about displaying

them with mice?"

Rachel immediately thought of the scrabbling sound she'd heard on the second floor of the bookstore. "In the window?"

"I have a whole set of adorable mice. They're woolen collectibles, hand-stitched by an artist in Louisiana. They're cute as a button. Let me show you."

Dinah led her around the corner to another illuminated class cabinet, and on the middle shelf was a little world of mice—a young mouse in pajamas, a mother mouse in a red wool coat pushing a tiny stroller with a baby mouse in a onesie. There was a mailman mouse, and a backpacking mouse, and a darling girl mouse in a pink coat and scarf carrying home a miniature Christmas tree.

"They're adorable," Rachel said, immediately thinking that these mice could be a fantastic display. "How much are they?"

"They're not inexpensive."

Rachel looked at the four-inch mice with their sweet expressions and dark bead eyes. "How much is the little boy mouse in pajamas?"

"Fifty dollars."

Rachel's heart fell. "And the girl mouse, with the Christmas tree?"

"I think she's seventy."

"So much," Rachel said regretfully.

"They're completely hand-stitched, by a well-known artist."

"I would buy them if I could," she answered, unable to justify spending even fifty on the little mouse boy in pajamas. "If I'm going to spend that much money, I should be buying books I could sell."

Dinah thought for a moment. "Have you tried the toy store? The one across from the diner? I think they sell Maileg toys."

Rachel shook her head. "I'm not familiar with the name."

"It's a Danish toy company. While my mice here are collectibles for adults, Maileg makes miniature stuffed animals for children. One of their top sellers is their stuffed mouse doll that comes in its own matchbox bed. They're very charming and usually priced between twenty-five and thirty dollars, although with retail markup, it's hard to know how the toy store will price them."

Rachel thanked her and walked back to the bookstore. She wanted a toy mouse, she did, but if she was going to be spending money, maybe she should be spending it on children's books.

Arriving back at the bookstore, she found it just as she'd left it. Atticus was working diligently at his small table, her stack of books were just as she'd left them. The only thing missing on the counter was her phone number. She arched a brow but said nothing, and just as she pulled her laptop toward her, her phone pinged with an incoming text.

She fished her phone out of her coat pocket and read the text. *"Now you have my number. And you can use it even if it's not an emergency. Atticus."*

She looked over at him, and he kept working away as if he hadn't just texted her. She stared at him for long minutes until he finally lifted his head. "Did you want something?" he asked.

His expression was so businesslike, so serious, and such a contradiction to his text that she slowly smiled.

Atticus was fun.

Rather irresistible, actually.

"No," she answered. "I'm good."

AN HOUR LATER, Atticus left and, once he was gone, she felt the bookstore was so quiet. True it was a Thursday, just before the Marietta Stroll, but other stores on Main Street had traffic. Maybe not heavy traffic, but the street was lined with cars, and people were walking around, only no one out shopping was entering the bookstore. Perhaps people didn't realize the store was actually open. Perhaps Paradise Books had been closed so long that everyone figured it wasn't going to reopen.

She stepped out onto the street and shivered at the icy blast of wind before stepping out into the street to look at the store, trying to see it the ways others saw it.

Tall brick building on the corner with big windows.

Window display still in need of inspiration. From outside, the interior of the store appeared fairly dark. The store needed new lighting, maybe some track lighting or warm spotlights to highlight the rich walnut bookshelves and handsome staircase.

If she kept the store, she'd need to invest in it.

New lighting, a new wireless router, update the children's reading room, update the downstairs bathroom, possibly recover some of the armchairs.

It would take some money but not a fortune, and businesses required upkeep. It was just a cost of doing business. She knew all the line items and deductions already. She knew what she could, and couldn't, write off.

But she couldn't write anything off, if there wasn't income. She needed to get people into the store. But first, she needed to make them notice the store. She'd start with a better window display.

Rachel went to the back room and poked around, looking for anything that she could use for displaying the Christmas books. She needed height. She needed something visually interesting. She wanted to stagger the books, so yes, a ladder would work, but so would a trunk, or boxes. Or... the wooden crates tucked behind cleaning supplies.

Rachel pulled three out. They were dusty and aged, but you could still make out some of the writing on the sides. COPPER MOUNTAIN BOTTLING WORKS on one, and MARIETTA MERCANTILE, MONTANA. Using her furniture polish, she wiped the crates down, removing a layer of grime and uncovered the faint words, DOUGLAS RANCH, PARADISE VALLEY, MT on the third. She wondered if the Douglas Ranch was connected to Sadie Douglas. If so, Sadie might be interested in this crate.

Rachel carried the crates to the window facing Main, and stacked them at angles so that she had more corners for displaying books. She set the brightest Christmas books upright on the crates, colorful covers facing out, and then shifted the poinsettias, putting them on either side of the crates. Standing outside she studied her new display. It still wasn't fabulous, in fact, it looked a little chaotic, but it was better than her first attempt. At least now you could see the books. That had to count for something.

Back in the store, she opened her laptop and researched window displays and read up on their importance and how it was the shop window that drives foot traffic.

A window display was supposed to highlight her brand's personality.

A proper window display was supposed to engage shoppers, and cause them to pause, look, and then enter the store where the sales personnel then closes the deal.

She wrinkled her nose. Oh dear. It hadn't crossed her mind that she'd need to be actually selling to people when they walked in. She might need someone with a sales personality.

Or someone who knew books and liked people.

When creating a window display one started with a story, based on a theme.

Rachel stopped reading again and rubbed her eyes, feeling as if she was back in a high school English class. Stories and themes. This was so not for her.

And then she told herself to buck up, this was just research, she couldn't be intimidated by an article on the internet. She continued reading. *Storytelling serves as one of the most critical business tools.*

She was to use her "storytelling prowess" to elevate her window.

And then she was to sketch her idea—

Rachel closed her laptop. *No.* No, no she couldn't come up with a story, and sketch out her windows, and then identify her focal points, and where her center line was. She had no center line, or focal points, sketching capability, or storytelling prowess. And she certainly had no idea how to deliver on the directive "To Be Bold in Every Way."

She'd spent her life *not* being bold.

She'd succeeded by working alone, quietly, under the radar for years.

But she did need to get people inside the store. And she obviously had to start building a relationship with customers.

Novak & Bartley regularly held client events. They had parties and golf tournaments and maybe she needed to host something, too.

Maybe she should have an open house, but it would have

to be soon.

Saturday was the Marietta Stroll.

Why not do it tomorrow night? She could host the party from five to seven, so that people, when leaving work, could just stop in.

RACHEL PRINTED FLYERS for her window and front door, and then walked an extra flyer up to Taylor at the Marietta Library. Taylor wasn't in, so Rachel left it with the woman at the reception desk. She texted Atticus about her party, and sent Zane a text, too. And then she planned her menu, and went grocery shopping, stopping by the Mercantile on her way home to see if they carried a Crock-Pot, and they did. It was a haul getting everything up to the third floor but Rachel was in a great mood as she twisted her hair into a knot, pushed up her sleeves, and got to work cooking and baking with Christmas carols playing in the background on her phone.

She sang along with the carols while she maneuvered baking sheets in and out of the small oven, and made her father's favorite tangy meatballs. She'd have a cheese and vegetable tray, her meatballs, and cookies and baked goods for dessert. She'd bought a couple bottles of wine, as well as some fizzy water, but maybe she'd ask Atticus to pick up some extra wine. It was so hard to know what people would drink, and how much they'd drink.

She went to bed tired but happy. It had been years since she'd thrown a party. She felt a little rusty but it was exciting to be doing something here, in Marietta, in her bookstore.

Atticus arrived Friday morning at nine with a tray of two coffees but no briefcase. He was dressed down, too, wearing jeans, and work boots and a chocolate-brown flannel shirt.

"No work today?" she asked him as he placed a coffee in front of her and took the other.

"You're serious about this party?" he answered.

"Yes. You saw my sign in the window. I'm having a holiday open house. Everyone's invited."

"Then we need to go get you a tree."

"What?"

"You can't have a holiday open house without holiday decorations, and what is more festive than a Christmas tree?"

"I was going to ask you to pick up a few more bottles of wine."

"I can do that, but decorations are essential."

She glanced around the bookstore, her frugal side not at all that convinced. "Do we really need a tree?"

"Don't you think it'd be beautiful?" He pointed to an area near the stairs. "You could get a really big one, and put it there, and it'd be a centerpiece—"

"A really big tree would cost a lot of money, and would require a lot more lights and decorations—"

"And that would cost a lot of money, too," he finished for her.

She shrugged uncomfortably. "What about a tabletop tree? Something that could sit here on the counter next to my food?"

"Boring. And you want something people can see from outside the store. Something that makes them want to come in."

"I've changed the display in the window that faces Main," she said helpfully.

"I saw the crates."

"And the books. There are six children's books now displayed, all with really bright illustrated covers."

"But the poinsettias."

"Why do you hate poinsettias?"

"I don't. But what do they have in common with children's books? Aren't they toxic?"

"If chewed on, but who is going to eat them?"

"If it were me, I would keep the display thematic. If you're displaying children's books, maybe add children's toys?"

"Not you, too." She groaned. "Themes will be the death of me."

"I have no idea what that means."

"Never mind. It's a very private, unfunny joke."

"If you want, I can go get a Christmas tree, and it'll be my contribution, along with a couple bottles of wine, to the party."

She glanced out the window. The sky was gray and thick

with high clouds. "It looks miserable out."

"I think we're going to see some snow."

She perked up at the mention of snow. The California girl in her still found snow rather miraculous. "And you're still comfortable getting a tree if it does snow?"

"It's not hard to drive in snow."

She was still looking out the window, trying to read the weather.

"I thought I'd drive to the Gallagher Tree Farm," he added. "See what it's like for myself."

Now he was just torturing her. "I wish I could go," she said, feeling a wistful pang.

"Why don't you?"

"Who will manage the store?"

Atticus choked on a smothered laugh. "I think you could put a sign in the window that said you'd be open at noon today. No one would mind."

"Could we really be back in a couple hours?"

"If we left now."

IT BEGAN TO snow on the drive to the tree farm. The first few flakes were slow and scattered. The wind that gusted from Yellowstone North through the Paradise Valley blew the fat lacy snowflakes every which way. Gradually the snow began to fall steadier, the flurries thickening, dusting the valley in white.

Rachel could hardly contain her excitement. She'd obviously seen snow before but she couldn't remember the last time she'd actually watched it snow. The powdery white flakes were magical and they piled lightly on tree branches like mounds of delicate meringue. She felt Atticus's gaze, and glanced at him, flashing him a delighted smile. Between baking for tonight's party, and this unexpected trip to the tree farm, she felt as if she was starting to get in the holiday spirit.

They turned off the highway and followed the signs for the tree farm, with the windshield wipers moving back and forth, softly swishing away the falling snow as they pulled into the farm's gravel parking lot. On the right side of the parking lot was a huge barn and in between the lot and the barn were dozens and dozens of cut trees. Some of the trees were upright in stands while others were stacked on the ground.

As they exited the car and headed toward the trees, a man in a thick parka and baseball cap approached. He held out his hand, introducing himself. "Sawyer Gallagher," he said, with an easy smile. "Welcome."

"You're Gallagher of Gallagher Tree Farms," Rachel said.

"I am."

"We've come for a tree," she said.

"You've come to the right place then. We grow all of our own trees, and carry pines, firs, and spruce. We also sell wreaths, and holiday decorations in the barn. You'll also find hot cider and cocoa in the barn, too, so head that way anytime you need to thaw out and warm up."

"Sounds good," Atticus answered.

"Have a look around, take your time, and let me know when I can help you."

Rachel tried to steer Atticus to the smaller trees, but he was having none of it. "This is my gift to you in the bookstore. You can't dictate my gift."

"We just don't have room for a fir tree in that store."

"You have plenty of room. Trust me."

"A bigger tree will require more lights and ornaments."

"I'm handling the tree. You're just along for the ride." And then he smiled to soften the words and she couldn't help smiling back.

"You are so bossy," she said.

"Maybe because you are very stubborn."

She laughed, and reached up to brush a smattering of snowflakes from her cheek. "It's really starting to come down."

"It's a perfect day."

"It really is," she agreed.

"This is why I want to have a restaurant here. I'm really comfortable in Montana. It's becoming a second home."

"Do you ever think you can live here?"

"At the Gallagher's? No. But Marietta? Yes."

She lightly punched his arm, near his bicep. "You are so ridiculous."

"But it makes you smile."

She nodded once, cheeks flushing. "Yes, it does," she admitted softly.

His eyes locked with hers, his blue gaze intent, and searching. There was so much warmth and kindness in his eyes. On one hand, he was a tall, rugged, intimidating man, and yet he treated her gently, as if she were delicate and valuable. She couldn't remember anyone ever treating her as if she were so valuable. Her eyes stung and a lump filled her throat.

She was falling for him. In fact, she may have already fallen for him.

They ended up with a ten-foot fir tree. It wasn't incredibly wide, just tall and slender, but still, it was so big that part of the tree hung over the back of the SUV after Sawyer and Atticus had tied it to the roof.

How on earth was this massive tree going to fit in her store? And more importantly how was this tree going to be decorated in time for the party tonight?

They didn't leave the tree farm until Atticus had filled the back seats with two wreaths, a half-dozen boxes of miniature white lights, and another half-dozen boxes of ornaments. She gasped at the total when Sawyer rang up the purchase, but Atticus didn't blink when he handed over his credit card. He didn't seem the least bit perturbed that he'd just spent hundreds of dollars when Rachel knew they could have purchased used ornaments for a lot less elsewhere.

"Stop making that face," Atticus said, as he shifted into drive. "I didn't rob a bank, and I committed no crime."

"I'm just uncomfortable with you spending that kind of money on a tree for my bookstore."

"If you're going to be throwing a party tonight, you might as well have the store decked out for the holidays. It's good for business and it's good for morale and I have no regrets."

"And who is going to do all the work of decorating the tree?"

"You and me."

"I have work to do."

He gave her an amused look. "What?"

"Well, I need to make the punch."

His lips twitched. "And what else?"

"I have to set up a card table and arrange the food."

He glanced at the clock on the dash. "It's only noon now. We have all afternoon."

"And I'm starving."

"I can pick up some sandwiches from the diner, and we can eat as we work."

"You have an answer for everything."

The corner of his mouth tilted. "I do."

IT STOPPED SNOWING midafternoon and Marietta's snowplows were out in full force, scraping streets clean. By dusk the Christmas lights were coming on, and Paradise Books glimmered with light from its magnificent Christmas tree.

Atticus had helped her move some of the furniture around and he'd managed to borrow a chafing dish and a silver tiered stand from the Graff for her meatballs and cookies. He returned to the hotel to shower and dress and she took the fastest shower ever, before dressing in trousers she'd paired with a red blouse and sparkly earrings. She hadn't brought anything too fancy with her but she felt pretty and festive as she descended the stairs and unlocked the door, ready for her guests.

She knew that people tended to be late, so she didn't worry when she was alone for the first twenty minutes. Rachel poured herself a glass of red wine and made small adjustments to her refreshment table before doing a walk around the towering Christmas tree, which they decorated with white lights and clear glass balls mixed in with some colored ornaments. It had struck Rachel as a little simplistic at the time of purchase, but now with the lights slightly dimmed, the tree looked so pretty.

She returned to the counter where she'd arranged the wine bottles and her fruit punch, a recipe her mom used to make. Rachel wasn't sure she'd gotten all the juice to soda ratio quite right but it tasted good and looked pretty with the orange slices and cranberries bobbing on top.

When it was quarter to six and still no one had yet come, she began to worry.

But then the door opened and it was Zane Nash, followed by Atticus and Troy and Taylor Sheenan. Zane's wife couldn't come as one of the kids were sick and she'd stayed home with the children, but Zane had brought wine, and Troy and Taylor had brought a large cinnamon scented candle wrapped in tissue. Rachel lit the candle and placed it on the counter next to the wine bottles and Atticus poured wine for everyone. After a bit Rachel invited Taylor to come up and see her little apartment on the third floor while the guys manned the door and greeted the other guests. Only no one else came.

She'd made food for fifty. Drinks for twice that, including her massive bowl of punch.

It was nearing seven and she eyed the chafing dish filled with meatballs and tried not to dwell on the fact that only a few had been eaten.

"Excellent punch," Atticus said, ladling some of the bright red liquid into his cup.

"Good to hear," she answered, smiling tightly, not wanting him to know just how disappointed she was.

"Your meatballs are very good, too."

"My grandmother Gerber's recipe. That was my mom's mom."

"The grandmother who loved Jessica Fletcher?"

Rachel's eyes stung and she blinked as she smiled hard. "The very one." Her voice had deepened and her heart felt banged up and she hated that she was getting so emotional.

She'd been so sure people would come.

Atticus stabbed a meatball with a toothpick, and popped it into his mouth and she turned away, unable to watch because he was the only one eating her food, and even with his most valiant efforts, there was no way Atticus could eat four dozen tangy meatballs.

She suddenly wished he wasn't here.

She wished he hadn't come tonight.

It would have been more bearable if he hadn't witnessed her humiliation.

Troy and Taylor approached with their coats, and Rachel's stomach fell. They were already leaving.

"I'm so glad you invited us," Taylor said.

"I'm so glad you came," Rachel answered.

"The bookstore looks fantastic," Troy said. "Lesley would be really pleased."

"She would," Taylor echoed. "And she'd be so happy to know you have the store open for the holidays. It was always her favorite time of the year."

Rachel was not going to cry. She was not even going to allow a single tear to well up. "I hope she'd be proud."

"We should take some pictures and send them to her," Taylor said, glancing at Troy. "She'd like that, wouldn't she?"

"Maybe another night during the holidays," Rachel said, not at all in the mood for photos right now.

"But the bookstore looks so pretty right now," Taylor

said.

Rachel's gaze went to Atticus where he was leaning against one of the upholstered chairs talking to Zane. "I'll have Atticus take some before I dismantle the buffet."

Troy followed her gaze. "He's not being pushy, is he?"

"He's been amazing," Rachel answered honestly. "He's been"—her voice cracked and she broke off, and bit hard into her lower lip to keep control—"supportive," she finished, when she could.

"I'm glad. He can be… intense," Taylor said, looking up at her husband.

Rachel didn't miss the exchanged glances. "I know he's interested in the bookstore. He's made an offer. But he's giving me time to figure out what I want to do, and I appreciate that."

"He's smart," Troy said. "And honest."

"You can trust him," Taylor added.

"And I do."

Troy and Taylor said their goodbyes then and left. Zane was next to go, and Atticus walked out with him, and she watched him go, feeling her heart tumble. Atticus was too handsome, as well as too smart. He was also too charismatic, and far too appealing.

She didn't date brilliant men with sexy smiles that resembled movie stars.

She didn't like larger than life personalities.

She didn't enjoy challenges that weren't spreadsheet or

tax related. She didn't enjoy challenges that involved emotions. And she certainly avoided challenges that came in the form of a devastatingly handsome male with endless options.

Rachel understood why she was attracted to Atticus—he was rather magnificent—but to be so impractical as to actually fall for him? To have real feelings for him? It was beyond foolish. It was desperate. Immature. Atticus treated her like a kid sister or a good friend, which would be fine if her own feelings were platonic. But they weren't and she didn't know how she'd even fallen for him. She'd thought she'd kept her guard up pretty well until the day she realized… there was no guard, and she did care for him, a great deal.

What had happened to her life and her routine? What happened to her most basic rules, the ones she organized her life by? These weren't new rules, but the ones that had guided her since college:

1. Set high, but achievable, goals
2. Work diligently toward goals
3. Regularly evaluate expectations
4. Weed out unrealistic expectations

She hadn't been vigilant about setting goals or maintaining realistic expectations since arriving in Montana, and because of that she'd not just fallen for Atticus, she'd set herself up for disappointment tonight, and tonight was nothing short of a disaster. Rachel blinked back tears, determined not to feel sorry for herself, but tonight's failure stung. She'd been so excited about the open house, certain this would be the event that relaunched Paradise Books. Naively, she'd imagined everyone would come. She'd thought that was how small towns worked—community and support. Everyone being there for everyone else.

She'd rushed into the party, and should have taken more time to prepare. She should have asked her few Marietta acquaintances to invite their friends. She should have taken an invite to the other businesses on Main, and made up a flyer for the library, not just for Taylor. Maybe she should have put a notice in the *Copper Mountain Courier*. The mistake was assuming people would come. The mistake was not having goals. The mistake was forgetting the importance of realistic expectations.

Chapter Seven

Rachel had just blown out the large cinnamon scented candle when the front door opened and Atticus stepped into the store carrying a shopping bag.

"Cleaning up is always easier with a separate pair of hands," he said, setting the paper bag on the counter.

"I'm fine."

He gave her a long, thoughtful look. "I don't think that's actually true."

"I'm not in the mood."

"For what?"

"For cheering up, or pity, or positive thinking. I know tonight was a massive failure. Please don't try to convince me it wasn't."

"Tonight you had stiff competition. A band from Missoula was performing across the street at Grey's. They're pretty popular around here." He emptied the shopping bags. "Plastic containers. We don't want to waste all that food."

She blinked, eyes burning. "That wasn't necessary."

"What were you going to put the food in?"

"I don't know."

"Neither did I. So let me help. No one enjoys cleaning up after a party all by themselves."

The lump in her throat grew. She swallowed hard, fighting exhausted tears. "It wasn't much of a party."

"I should have done more to get people here."

"It wasn't your party. You don't need to feel responsible."

"I know."

Her chin lifted and she met his gaze. "Atticus, don't complicate things, please. We're not on the same team."

"We're not enemies, either," he said quietly. "Just because I'm fighting for this spot, doesn't mean I'm fighting *you*. I don't like seeing you hurt. I don't want to see you hurt."

Her pride in tatters, she gave a short nod. "Okay."

"Where should I start?"

Rachel turned to face the platters overflowing with cookies and cakes and cheese and crackers and fruit, and then there was the chafing dish of meatballs. "Maybe there?" she asked, nodding at the chafing dish.

"You have a lot of meatballs."

"I went overboard."

"At least we know you commit. Commitment is a good thing."

"Unless you are committing to the wrong thing, and then it's a problem."

"I don't see that being something you would do. You're

pretty savvy."

"I wish I was. But the truth is, I don't even know what I'm doing anymore. I don't know what I mean to do with the store. I have a really good job in California and there's no way I can run Paradise Books from there. And, let's face it, the store does not have enough revenue to pay for staff, not unless I get very creative very fast."

"You do have that apartment upstairs. You can always rent that out. It'd provide some income, and maybe pay for staffing for the store."

"So keep my real job and keep the bookstore?"

"Why not? It's doable, if you can get the mail-order business going."

She hated all the emotions washing through her. It was too much emotion. She felt like she was losing control. "I thought you wanted this place."

"I do, but I don't want to get it by being underhanded. Far better to acquire the bookstore when you're ready to sell than to push you into something you'll later regret."

She sniffled. "You think I'll regret selling the store?"

"I think it matters more to you than you care to admit."

Her chest ached with emotion. Her eyes were hot and gritty. Something inside her felt slightly unhinged and she looked away, focused on the Christmas tree. At least it was a nice tree. "I'm glad you insisted on a big tree. It's beautiful."

"Your party was beautiful."

"What about your next Galveston? Aren't you starting to

get a little impatient with this whole thing?"

"The restaurants I have are doing quite well. My future doesn't hinge on this one location."

"I don't understand you," she said after a long moment. "You should be making this harder for me, not easier."

"Is that what friends do?"

Her heart thumped. Her throat ached. She wanted so many things just then that the need overwhelmed her. "You're a good friend," she answered huskily. "Thank you."

"You're welcome. Now let's divide and conquer or we'll be doing this all night."

It took them forty minutes to carry everything up and package the food. Her refrigerator and freezer were small so she could only store perishables like the fruit, the artichoke spinach dip and her meatballs, and so she stacked the plastic containers of baked goods in the corner on the counter. Atticus rolled up his shirt sleeves and washed the now empty dishes and platters while she dried. They didn't speak but the silence only served to make it feel even more intimate. Rachel tried to think of something to say, but it wasn't until they'd finished the last dish that she found her voice.

"Thank you," she said, trying not to be flustered by the intimacy of their domestic tasks. Atticus was a good partner. He had a way of making her feel supported... even cherished. "I'm glad you insisted on helping. I would have been miserable doing this by myself."

He finished wiping down the counters before returning

the sponge to the sink. "I wouldn't have left you to do this on your own. It was a big job."

"My commitment to meatballs and all," she said wryly.

He flashed her a smile. "And I find your commitment commendable."

"You're very good at this sort of thing."

He wiped his hands dry on a dish towel. "I have spent a lot of time in restaurant kitchens. You learn a thing or two over the years."

She shook her head, blushing. "I didn't mean the tidying up, although you do that very well. I meant, dealing with me and all my emotions."

"You're not hard to deal with, and you're not that emotional."

"I was upset tonight."

"You were disappointed."

"I hate being disappointed." She leaned against the counter and looked away. "I work very hard to make sure I'm not disappointed."

"You can't escape disappointment. It's just part of life."

The heaviness in her chest made her aware of all the emotions she was battling to suppress but the emotions were bubbling up, and it wasn't just tonight that was undoing her, but the past month and how hurt she'd been after being passed over for the last promotion. What had happened to her sense of accomplishment? She felt horrifyingly fragile… vulnerable… and she didn't like those feelings, at all.

"Would you want a glass of wine?" she asked. "We have an awful lot."

"I'll take a glass of the red that we'd opened earlier."

She grabbed two of the freshly washed glasses and the shiraz and hesitated, glancing to the couch in the small living area. It was a small area, and a small couch but it was the only furniture in the sitting area. "Do you mind if we sit? It's a cozy couch."

"I'm ready to relax. It's been a busy day."

"Yes, and my feet are killing me."

Once they sat, he did the honors of pouring and she squished herself into the farthest end of the couch and watched him. He was lovely to look at. Lovely to be near. This was a problem. "Do you cook?" she asked, trying to fill the silence.

"I can do okay."

"Do you cook when you're home?"

"Not enough. I tend to eat out a lot. But then, I travel a lot. It doesn't make sense to stock the fridge and then be gone for the next week." He handed her a wineglass and then settled back in the couch, one muscular arm extended along the back of the couch, his fingers very close to her shoulder. "The travel is getting old, though. I'm starting to think I'm ready for a change."

"You don't have a girlfriend or significant other back in Houston, do you?"

He shook his head. "I don't really do serious relationships. The last woman I saw steadily was Nikki, and that was a year ago."

"What happened?" she asked, before grimacing. "You don't have to answer that."

"My flight out of Chicago got canceled and I couldn't make it back in time for her company's holiday party. She was tired of going solo to places because I'm rarely home. We had a tense conversation and then broke up."

"Were you devastated?"

He gave her an amused look. "I liked Nikki, but we weren't going to settle down and have babies."

"Do you even want to have babies?"

The corner of his mouth curved. "I note your sarcasm, Rachel, and yes, eventually I want a family. Don't you?"

She opened her mouth, closed it. To be honest, she didn't ever think about marrying and having kids. She'd never met anyone who made her want to marry. "It's not one of my goals."

"I don't know that it has to be a goal."

"It's not something I see, though." She shrugged, embarrassed. "I've had a vision board since my senior year of high school, and it's helped me focus and work toward my future. I never included marriage or family because those aren't necessarily attainable goals—"

"Why not?"

"They depend on other people. I don't like goals that hinge on others."

"So marriage is out."

She laughed at his expression. "I don't know if it's out, but it's not important right now."

"What is important?"

"I thought it was becoming Novak & Bartley's first female director, and then their first female partner, but that is probably not going to be an option."

"Why?"

Her desire to laugh faded. "It's not a place where dreams come true." Rachel cringed as she said the words. She'd meant to be flippant but it sounded hollow in her ears.

He reached for the bottle and topped off her wineglass and then his own. "Why remain at a place that doesn't make you happy?"

Her shoulders twisted. "I'm paid well. There is security, as long as I don't want too much."

"But obviously you want more."

She rotated her goblet, swirling the wine, watching it splash the sides of the glass. "I just don't understand how, when I've done everything right, it feels all wrong."

"Tragically, life isn't a math equation that can be solved."

She grimaced. "Can I tell you something that I've never told anyone?"

"Please do."

Rachel took a sip of wine for liquid courage. "I took golf lessons." She paused, thinking about those lessons. "For two years, I took private golf lessons so I'd be ready for the day I was invited to attend Novak & Bartley's annual golf tournament. It's their biggest client appreciation event—they do two a year, the big summer party, and the Holiday Classic—and they invite all their VIPs to attend, as well as their managers, directors and partners. I've been a manager for three years and still haven't been invited. But at least I learned to play golf."

ATTICUS HATED THE tightness in his chest.

She had a way of making him feel things he didn't want to feel. She presented complications that were completely unnecessary. And yet, if he were ready to settle down, and ready to find a wife, she would be exactly the kind of woman he'd want. A smart, no-nonsense woman like Rachel. A woman whose confessions were painfully honest, and painfully real.

Normally such confessions would have him wanting distance, and yet with her, he wanted more closeness.

More of her.

"Did you buy your own clubs?" he asked, trying not to focus on her full soft mouth, or the wistful expression that made her lips curve. It wasn't easy when her lower lip trembled and he wanted to haul her closer to him, and kiss that lovely quivering lip.

She grimaced, nose wrinkling. "The clubhouse had a really good after Christmas sale."

That didn't surprise him, either. She understood the value of money.

He pictured her on the green with her clubs, long blonde hair in one of her high ponytails. "You're disappointed in your management team," he said, determined to keep the conversation moving so that he could ignore the impossible, uncomfortable emotion filling him. She was imperfectly perfect, or perfectly imperfect and she should be sitting at his side, his arm around her, her body tucked against his. She made him want to fight her battles for her, and yet it was also the last thing she'd tolerate.

"I was sure I'd be given the chance," she answered. "I knew what was required, and I did what was required. It didn't cross my mind that two plus two would not equal four."

"See, you trusted your math facts."

She smiled crookedly but the smile didn't reach her eyes. "I did, and what I learned is that it wasn't numbers that let me down, but people."

"Not all people will disappoint you."

She didn't answer but he could see from her expression she didn't believe him, and actually, she was right. People made mistakes. People did disappoint. But it wasn't always intentional. He thought of his last case, the one that had gone to trial, the one that had made him walk away from litigation forever. A day didn't go by where he wished he could change the outcome, protect Manuel from a justice system that wasn't always just.

"Have you thought of interviewing elsewhere?" he asked.

"I hadn't, not until last week. But it's something I'm thinking about now."

"You didn't want to have to go somewhere else," he said.

"I didn't. I thought I'd be there forever."

"And then in the middle of all this, you discover Lesley has given you Paradise Books. That must have seemed providential."

"Or a distracting temptation," she answered, drawing her legs up under her and shifting to completely face him. "If I were a book enthusiast, or had nurtured a secret dream of one day owning my own business in an adorable small town, I would be in heaven. But my dream was to be a corporate accountant, with a big firm, doing big business."

"You are using past tense."

Shadows flickered in her eyes. "I'm confused."

"There are other big accounting firms. You're not trapped at Novak."

"But leaving feels defeatist."

Again he thought of Manuel, and the sentencing, and how that one case had forced him to not just reevaluate his career, but his values and his sense of self-worth. He'd failed Manuel, and he'd failed Manuel's family, and it had taken him a long time to even want to practice law again. "Change is an inherent part of life. Sometimes we welcome it. Sometimes we resist it. But change happens, with or without our permission."

"My problem is that change *isn't* happening."

"So create change. *You* be the one to change." Then he did what he'd been wanting to do all night. He leaned toward her, closing the distance between them, and kissed her. It was a light kiss, tentative, giving her a chance to pull away. She didn't, she leaned in, her lips softening against his. She tasted of the shiraz they were drinking and it was heady, making him want more. Reaching up, he brushed his knuckles across her warm cheek, her skin petal smooth. Desire rushed through him, and he deepened the kiss, parting her lips, to kiss her more thoroughly.

RACHEL COULDN'T REMEMBER the last time she'd been kissed like this—with hunger and heat, but also this lovely tenderness that made her feel wanted, and protected. She felt as if she couldn't get close enough to him and leaned in to the kiss, loving the way his arm wrapped around her and pulled her tighter so that she was practically sprawling across his lap. Atticus was as strong and muscular as he looked, his body hard against hers, and she shuddered with pleasure as he stroked the length of her back, finding nerve endings that had been forgotten in oh, forever.

Did kissing always feel this good, or was it just Atticus that made her want more? Because she did want more. Need and want washed through her and she placed a hand on his chest, his warmth and strength impossibly seductive.

Atticus shifted her, drawing her more firmly across his lap, the pressure of his mouth more insistent, his teeth catching at her lower lip, sending darts of exquisite sensation throughout her. She stopped worrying about control and boundaries, wanting to be swept away, wanting to escape smart, sensible Rachel with her exhausting goals and endless plans.

She was breathless and dazed when he finally lifted his head. She blinked, trying to clear her vision, even as she could feel the steady drumming of Atticus's heart against the palm of her hand.

His blue eyes burned brightly. He looked impossibly handsome as he smiled down at her. "You are full of surprises," he said.

She blushed. "You're the one with expert lips."

He smiled, amused, and then his smile faded and he brushed his thumb across her sensitive lips. "I think I just like kissing you."

Her heart did a double beat. "I've tried so hard to keep you at arm's length. I even tried to hate you. It didn't work."

"Why hate me?"

"Two dogs, one bone, that sort of thing."

"There are other bones," he answered, dipping his head to place a kiss on her forehead, and then the tip of her nose.

"Yes, but you really want this place."

"Not as much as I want you happy."

"Kissing you made me happy."

"A note to self," he said, kissing her on the mouth, with a slow, warm lingering kiss, "which makes me wonder if we're going about this wrong."

"Going about what wrong?"

"You, me, the bookstore."

She still felt deliciously fuzzy from the kisses, and she wasn't sure she was following. Correction, she knew she wasn't following. She wasn't able to focus at all. "I'm afraid kissing you has fogged my brain. What are you saying?"

"We shouldn't be fighting each other. We should team up. Partner with each other."

Rachel slid off his lap and reclaimed her spot on the small couch. A moment ago she felt deliciously alive, humming with lovely sensation, but the lovely warmth was fading and she just felt confused.

"Maybe we've been approaching this business transaction all wrong," he added. "Maybe we're supposed to do something together."

"How?"

"We create a partnership here in Montana, combine our interests—"

"But our interests are in opposition."

"Are they? Why can't we do something jointly with the bookstore?"

Rachel jumped off the couch and crossed to the kitchen where she leaned against a counter. Her pulse was thudding but not with good emotion. She struggled to contain the panic.

"I don't think…" She swallowed hard, and tried again. "I don't know. I'm not sure this is a good idea. We have different goals. We want different things."

"I'm simply saying I think we should have a conversation about how we could work together, that's all. We get along well. I think we'd be good partners."

"Business partners."

"Not necessarily just business."

He'd just made her feel the most wonderful things. She couldn't remember when she'd last felt so alive, or optimistic, but this, what he was suggesting, filled her with unease, if not downright dread.

"I'm overwhelming you," he said.

"A little," she admitted.

"It's just a thought."

She nodded, and forced herself to smile. "I'm just tired. It's been a long day."

"You're right." He rose and went to her, and kissed her on the forehead. "I probably should have waited."

"No, I'm glad you brought it up. It's good to know what you're thinking," she answered, because it was, and now she could be prepared, and cautious.

She'd loved kissing him tonight, but she was horrified by his suggestions. He had plans, and so did she, and there was safety in plans. There was a reason for their plans.

Downstairs at the door, he kissed her good night, kissing her with the same heat and passion he'd shown upstairs, kissing her until her skin prickled and her veins felt like they were full of honey and hot wine, and when the kiss ended, he stepped away and gave her a faint smile.

"You are hard to resist, Rachel Mills," he said before lifting his coat from the coatrack and walking out in the night.

Rachel closed the door behind him, locked it, and then stood at the door a moment, fist pressed to her mouth as she watched him disappear. She liked him. She liked him more than she'd liked anyone in years, and tonight he'd made her feel pleasure and hope and happiness, but now she wondered if she'd imagined all those good feelings. Emotions were dangerous, and not to be trusted.

She'd come to Marietta for the bookstore. She'd come to make decisions, and figure out her future, not fall in love with Atticus and throw caution to the wind.

TAYLOR SHEENAN ARRIVED not long after Rachel opened the bookstore the next day.

"I couldn't sleep very well last night," Taylor said. "I feel really bad about not doing more to support your party."

"It's not your fault. It's mine—"

"It's not your fault. You've only just arrived in town and you don't know anyone yet. It's not easy being the new person in town. I know, because when I first moved here, it took me a long time to feel like I belonged."

"Really?"

She nodded. "If I hadn't met Troy, I don't know if I would have stayed in Marietta. He has a huge family, five brothers, and they're all married. I should have reached out to them and asked them to come to your open house."

"Grey's Saloon had a crowd last night," Rachel said.

"They always get a crowd when they have popular bands."

Rachel hadn't even realized Grey's was having a band in until Atticus mentioned it last night, but then, it hadn't crossed her mind that there would be competition, either. "Lesson learned," she said lightly. "Next time I'll be better prepared."

"I was hoping you'd say that."

"Say what?"

"Next time. So you will do another party?"

"Well, I'm sure I will… someday."

"How about tonight, during the Marietta Stroll?"

Rachel frowned. "If I can't compete with Grey's, how can I compete with the stroll, although to be perfectly honest, I don't fully understand the stroll."

"It's Marietta's annual Christmas event. It's half street party, half festival. All the stores on Main Street stay open, and there are horse drawn wagons through town, the lighting of the big tree at the courthouse, plus Santa and the gingerbread competition at the Graff. It's the perfect time for everyone to rediscover the bookstore."

"I'm not so sure Marietta cares about the bookstore anymore."

"Maybe they don't really know you've reopened. Maybe you need more of a presence."

"I redid the window display, on both sides."

"And you did a great job. The store looked gorgeous last night with your Christmas tree and holiday buffet. Now we just need to get people inside."

"You really think my windows are enough?" Rachel asked, suddenly anxious as she peeked at the colorful children's books balancing on vintage wooden crates. It wasn't a Macy's window, but it was better than the Valentine display that had been there for nearly three years.

"I do."

"And you think I should participate in the stroll tonight?"

"Most definitely. Everyone up and down Main Street will be staying open now until the end of the stroll, which typically ends around nine."

"Do any of the businesses serve wine or food?"

"They do, and this would be the perfect occasion if you still had any party leftovers."

"Taylor, I could feed an army with all my meatballs, cookies, and cakes."

"Sounds like you're having another party." Taylor smiled. "And this time cleanup will be a breeze. There won't be hardly any food or drink left after the stroll ends."

TAYLOR WAS RIGHT.

The Marietta Stroll was a busy, crowded event and thanks to the frosted sign, WE'RE OPEN, painted on her windows by a friend of Taylor's, people flocked in. But even before the stroll kicked off, deliveries were made to the bookstore, gifts from other businesses on Main Street. Risa sent flowers, Sage sent salted caramels, and Rachel Vaughn delivered a tray of gingerbread cookies in the shape of books, each book iced and then wrapped in clear cellophane.

And just when Rachel Mills didn't think she could handle another sweet surprise, Sadie Douglas arrived with her husband Rory and climbed into her window and went to work moving the crates around, and removed some books, and then lifted a set of hardback books from the trunk. The books were all stuck together, possibly glued, and Sadie placed this on top of a crate she'd turned upside down, making it taller.

Rachel bit her tongue to keep from saying anything that would sound ungrateful, and yet she didn't understand what Sadie was doing, but Rory clearly did because he kept handing her tools and then connecting lights, and adjusting another crate so that the odd book thingy was higher.

"That's interesting," Rachel finally said, trying to hide her panic because Sadie had completely destroyed her window display. Now there were only three of the picture books in the windows with the crates and the massive set of hardback books that now had lights shining out of the back.

"Not done yet," Sadie said, flashing Rachel a smile.

"Mmm," Rachel answered, still not reassured because Sadie's own store window was beautiful while Paradise Books's front window reminded Rachel of a yard sale.

Sadie was now sprinkling faux powdered snow across the top of a crate, in front of the hardback books, before adding a small figure. Sadie fiddled about another few minutes before nodding her head. "Perfect," she said, climbing out of the window and dusting her knees off. "Rachel, go outside, have a look, and tell me what you think."

Outside, Rachel stood in front of the window facing Main Street and blinked in surprise as she realized that the set of hardback books was actually a street of nineteenth-century townhomes, and each spine was a different house, with miniature windows glued to the spines, and unique doors on the base of each book. Some of the houses had window boxes and others had little slate roofs. One had steps. Another had a gate for a carriage. And there in front of one of the handsome wooden doors was a little mouse dressed in a white shirt with a green vest, just like the mouse on *Mouse's Christmas Gift*.

"It's a mouse town," she said in wonder, thinking she couldn't wait to show Atticus this, before realizing he hadn't been in yet today, which was unusual.

"I heard via the grapevine you wanted a Nativity set and a mouse," Sadie said, standing next to her and admiring her handiwork. "I couldn't find a Nativity scene, but I made a mouse for you. I hope you like it."

"I do. It's perfect," Rachel answered, bowled over by Sadie's thoughtfulness.

THE STROLL WAS just as perfect, with dozens of families streaming in and out, while a quartet of Dickens carolers sang outside on the doorstep. Nearly everyone that came in snagged a cookie and sampled the punch, before wandering around the store, pausing to admire the fresh fragrant Christmas tree. A number of people asked about the Christmas books in the window and Rachel realized that if she was going to keep the store open, she would need to order in children's books like the ones in the window display. But everyone she talked to was delighted the store was open, and shared stories with her about Lesley. Lesley was loved and missed, and Rachel vowed to pass the messages on.

The only person who didn't come by was Atticus and Rachel tried to tell herself it was fine, but the fact that she missed him as much as she did meant she wasn't really fine. It was just that he was the one person she'd expected to put in an appearance, and when he didn't, she wasn't sure what to do with her disappointment. His absence made her realize she was already attached to him, and she had strong feelings for him—terrible, wonderful feelings—and she'd never be able to think of Marietta without thinking of him.

But finally the crowds from the stroll dispersed and the traffic on the street dwindled to nothing. She'd just begun to throw all the leftovers away when Atticus arrived, and her pulse quickened when he walked through the front door.

"I didn't think I was going to see you tonight," she said, feeling ridiculously relieved to finally see him.

"It's been a tough day. I've had to spend most of it on the phone looking for a new head chef for the San Francisco Galveston."

"Oh, dear. That doesn't sound fun."

"It wasn't, and I missed the stroll. Was it as wonderful as everyone said?"

"People seemed happy, and the bookstore was never empty."

"I take it you never left the store."

She shook her head. "But I wasn't lonely. All the Sheenans came to meet me, and there are a lot of them."

"Yes, there are." He smiled. "Let's stroll down Main Street before all the lights have been turned off."

She did like the sound of that and quickly bundled up and locked the door. Atticus took her hand as they walked down the middle of the street because cross traffic was still blocked off. Some of the stores still glowed with lights, while others had gone dark for the night. They walked the length of Main Street and were starting back when Atticus took her on a detour, heading down Third Street and then over onto Church where they walked another block before stopping in the middle of a residential area.

"That's your house," Atticus said.

"My house?" she echoed, confused.

"Your mom's house. The one where your mom and grandparents lived in Marietta."

Rachel blinked, shocked. "This was Mom's house?"

He nodded.

She couldn't believe it. "How did you find out?"

"I'm good at finding out things."

Her gaze swept the small white, single-story house. The house still had its original wooden windows, and a narrow front porch. The current owners had strung Christmas lights along the edge of the steeply pitched roof, the white icicle light variety, and red-and-white candy canes lined the narrow cement walkway. It was tidy but sweet, and not far from the schools at the end of the street. "Mom would have been able to walk to school every day," she said.

"Lesley's childhood home was on the same street, just a block south, closer to St. James. I have a feeling they walked to school together."

His words made her ache, and she blinked hard, clearing the stinging sensation from her eyes. She hadn't thought of Mom in so long and now it seemed like her mother was everywhere. "Marietta would have been a wonderful place to grow up. It's reassuring. Makes me believe she had a good life. I hope she did."

"I think she was happy here," he answered. "She certainly had good friends. Just look at Lesley."

Rachel nodded. "I think she was happy with my dad, too."

"How was she as a mom?"

"Loving. Funny. I think she used to laugh a lot." She blinked hard, fighting tears. "Back before she was sick."

"I have a feeling you remember more than you think you do."

"I don't want to remember it wrong."

"Just love her, and you won't get it wrong."

She exhaled hard. "That's where it gets tricky." She looked at him and then looked away. "I was mad at her for a long time. Mad at her for dying. Mad at her for making my high school years all about her." Her voice broke and she drew a shuddering breath. "I have hated myself for that. I'm not a very loving person."

Atticus reached out and carefully adjusted her knit cap on her head, pulling the edge down on one side and then the other. "You were a girl that lost her mom. Why wouldn't you be angry?"

"But at her? How was it her fault?"

"It wasn't, but she was your mom. She was supposed to make you feel safe, and suddenly she's ill and you realize that the world is a dangerous place."

His words were like a shot to the heart. She opened her

mouth, closed it, pain suffusing her. She'd been alone with her mom when she died and the grief had been overwhelming.

What did she do with so much grief?

"I don't like emotions," she said huskily.

"I can understand that. They're tough for you. I mean, where do you put them on your vision board?"

She laughed even as the pinch in her chest deepened, because many a truth was said in jest, and he was oh, so very right. There was no room in her life for emotions. She'd made sure of that. "You're beginning to know me a little too well."

"Fortunately, I like who you are."

That made her chest tighten with yet more emotion. She was feeling so much, possibly too much. And yet, being here, seeing her mother's former house, was wonderful. Glancing at the small house, she could almost see her mom sitting on the front porch in summer, and skipping down the steps on her way to a date. "This is pretty cool," she whispered. "Thank you. I feel like you've given a little bit of Mom back to me."

Chapter Eight

Atticus took Rachel's hand as they walked back to the bookstore. Rachel had gone quiet and he glanced down at her, thinking things were definitely not simple anymore.

He filled the silence by talking to her about his family, and how they'd spent holidays in Texas. His grandparents owned a beach house on Galveston and they'd often celebrate Thanksgiving and Christmas there—

"That's why you've named your restaurants Galveston," she interrupted.

He nodded. "I have great memories of the island. My dad's family has lived there since the late 1880s, and were there during the Galveston hurricane of 1900."

"I've never heard of the storm."

"It's considered the deadliest natural disaster in American history. Thousands died, and nearly every house on the island was damaged or destroyed. Many people moved to Houston. My dad's family stayed."

"Do you ever feel like you should be there?"

He shook his head. "My brother is there—"

"You have a brother?"

"I haven't mentioned him?"

"*No.*"

"Holden was an oops baby, created on my parents fifteenth anniversary getaway."

"Sorry to interrupt again," Rachel said. "But isn't Holden another literary name?"

"Holden Caulfield, from Salinger's *Catcher in the Rye.*"

"Your mother really does love her books."

"In this case, Holden was partially my father's responsibility. Salinger's novel was his favorite book from high school." Atticus smiled wryly. "He likes to tell me he got the better name, but obviously I disagree."

She smiled. "So what does Holden do in Galveston?"

"He's a petroleum engineer. It runs in the family. My father is, too."

"But not you?"

"I've been the challenging one," he admitted. "From birth, I've had my own ideas, and I think it was a relief for them when I headed off to college."

"You enjoy the battle."

"I enjoy problem solving. My brain responds well to puzzles and strategizing."

"I don't like competition," she said, "but I've never minded working hard, and I like a good challenge."

"Me, too. As soon as someone says it can't be done, I want to prove them wrong," he said, stopping in front of the bookstore front door.

"I'm not usually influenced by others. I don't tend to care what others think. I care what I think. It it's something I want to do, then I'm going to do it."

"Which is why you've been taking your time trying to figure out what you want to do about Paradise Books."

"Exactly."

"AND WHY YOU don't want my input on the bookstore."

"I never said that." He gave her a look and she grimaced. "I just know what I can handle, and what's realistic considering my career doesn't allow much travel, or flexibility," she added.

"You're not locked into a lifetime of drudgery at Novak & Bartley."

"I never said it was drudgery."

"They don't respect you."

She crossed her arms over her chest, jaw tight, expression mutinous. "I don't badmouth your company. Don't badmouth mine."

"I'm on your team, Rachel."

She looked away from him, toward the glow of the streetlight. For a long moment neither of them spoke and the silence wasn't comfortable but he wasn't going to back down. She wasn't appreciated where she was in Irvine. She deserved better. It was time she put herself first.

Abruptly she rose on tiptoe and pressed a kiss to his cheek. "Thank you for showing me Mom's house."

"My pleasure."

"Sleep well," she said.

"You, too," he answered, "and sleep in tomorrow if you can. It's Sunday. Take some time for yourself. A lot of stores don't open on Sundays here. You don't have to open, or be open all day."

"What would I do if I didn't open the store?" she asked, tightening her scarf.

"I have an idea or two. Why don't I text you in the morning and see how you feel?"

"Why don't you tell me your ideas now and I'll tell you if I'm interested?"

"It's easier to be rejected by a text."

She laughed, the sound bubbling with warmth. "Do you really think I'd reject you?"

"If you didn't like my suggestions."

"Not going to argue with you on that." She was still smiling up at him, looking angelic beneath the glow of the old-fashioned streetlight with her golden hair and bright eyes. "There's a reason I'm still single at my age. I'm a lot of work, and I know it."

"You're not a lot of work. You're just you, and you don't have to change being you for anyone." He leaned down and kissed her cheek. "I'll text you in the morning."

Rachel couldn't sleep in, even if she wanted to. She'd been an early bird her entire life, often doing her best studying while it was still dark outside. She woke early Sunday morning, and drank her first cup of coffee in bed, before carrying her second cup around the second floor of the bookstore examining the shelves. She'd heard that scrabbling sound again as she'd been making coffee and she was determined to find the mouse or rodent or whatever it was that was making itself a little too comfortable on the second floor.

As she wandered between the rows, the fiction section organized alphabetically by author, she passed the *A*s with its numerous Alcotts and Austens, moving on to *B*s and *C*s before reaching the *D*s where the Charles Dickens book had fallen to the floor. She paused there, and drew the different Dickens titles out, checking behind the antique books for signs of rodent life, but everything was clean and clear. She moved on through the shelves, turning one corner and then another before coming to a row in the *T*s where a tall, slender book was sticking out.

Rachel went to push the book back in, but then she noticed the title. *The Father Christmas Letters*. A Christmas book. She pulled it out and examined the colorful cover. The author was J.R.R. Tolkien. Wasn't that the author of *The Lord of the Rings*?

She carried the book to an armchair by the window, placed her coffee on the windowsill and leafed through the pages, which were filled with dates and handwritten letters and quirky illustrations. She skipped the introduction, going straight to the first letter dated 1925 and it was all about Father Christmas's recent move and how the North Polar Bear wasn't there to help and Father Christmas was having quite a hard time of it. She was highly entertained by the story, and she studied the illustration accompanying the letter, before turning the page, reading the next letter dated 1926. The letters were stories about Father Christmas's life at the North Pole. After reading several letters, Rachel flipped back to the front of the book to read the introduction. *The Father Christmas Letters* had been collected and published after Tolkien's death by his son, and edited by his daughter-in-law. The letters and illustrations spanned twenty years and were copies of the actual letters Tolkien had written to his children every year for twenty years. What a treasure, she thought, closing the back cover, and it made her wonder, what other treasures were here in Paradise Books? She really should find out.

But in the meantime, what was she to do about the bookstore mouse? She hadn't seen any damage. Maybe it was a literary mouse. Maybe it just loved books. In that case, she should welcome the company.

Smiling, she carried her cup and book upstairs, and did a search on the Tolkien book, and was excited to see the copy she had ranged in value from sixty to ninety-five dollars. Nice. There was value in this store. She just had to find the books that were special and get those onto one of the national databases. Maybe she should start with Christmas books. What else might Lesley have bought that was tucked away?

Still online, she did a search for "classic Christmas stories" and was rewarded with numerous suggestions, with the most popular being *A Christmas Carol* by Charles Dickens, followed by *'Twas the Night Before Christmas*, *The Gift of the Magi*, *The Nutcracker and the Mouse King*, and *A Christmas Memory* by Truman Capote. There were more suggestions, too, like *The Life and Adventures of Santa Claus* by Frank Baum, and *Christmas in the Big Woods* by Laura Ingalls Wilder, and *The Greatest Gift*, which became the basis for Frank Capra's Christmas film classic, *It's a Wonderful Life*.

Rachel scribbled all the suggested titles down and went in search of them on the second floor, and was delighted to discover she had all but the one by Laura Ingalls Wilder. Rachel took the books, photographed them, input the details into the online site she'd found that specialized in antique and collectible books and then created a display with them on a round table not far from the front door. Lesley had collected the classics. Surely there was someone out there that would love to add these books to their collection. It was time to fight technology with technology.

She was still working intently hours later when her phone buzzed with a text from Atticus. *"Hungry? The Graff does a popular Santa Brunch. I can put our names in for a one o'clock reservation."*

Brunch at fancy restaurants had never been her thing but

her pulse had quickened when she saw Atticus's name on her phone. She liked him. Very much.

He texted again. *"Santa is here. You know you want to see him."*

She shook her head, amused, and then glanced at her table with the classic Christmas stories and thought he was right. She would enjoy a festive Christmas something, especially if it included Atticus, and maybe a glimpse of the Graff Hotel's Santa Claus.

"Make the res," she typed. *"I'll see you at one."*

Rachel showered and changed into the red blouse she'd worn for her open house party, pairing the blouse with dark skinny jeans and her favorite pair of ankle boots. She considered driving to the hotel but thought the fresh air and walk would do her good, so she set off fifteen minutes early.

The air was cold—bracing—and she drank in great breaths, filling her lungs, clearing her head. The sky was blue with just a few high clouds. The sun shone brightly down on the dome of the historic courthouse, and Copper Mountain rose, majestic, behind all.

It was such a pretty town. She was still a stranger here, but it was growing on her, the tidy downtown surrounded by old neighborhoods lined with Victorians and Queen Annes. Although Marietta looked small, she'd learned that there were some big businesses operating in the valley, from ranching dynasties to entrepreneurs and media conglomerates. She ought to find out which accounting firms were here. It'd be interesting to know who was doing business in Paradise Valley, not that she was thinking of relocating here, but it was always good to know who the competition was.

Atticus was waiting for her on the hotel's front steps. He smiled as she climbed them.

"You didn't have to wait out here," she said, as he gave her a hug and then held the door open for her.

"I know, but it's a beautiful day. Look at Copper Mountain."

"Why do they call it Copper Mountain? Did they really find copper?"

"From what I understand, not very much. Marietta enjoyed a brief mining boom, and most of the buildings on Main Street were built during that ten-year boom, but it turned out to be a small vein and it wasn't long before it ran out."

"What happened to Marietta?"

"It declined. By the 1920s Marietta was almost a ghost town. If it weren't for the ranchers and cattle in the valley, Marietta wouldn't have survived. The Graff was closed for over twenty years. Troy was the one responsible for bringing it back."

"Troy Sheenan?"

Atticus nodded. "This is his labor of love. It nearly broke him."

"Doesn't sound like a smart investment," she said.

"It wasn't just an investment. He did it because the hotel

was his mom's favorite place. She died when he was a senior in high school."

"Like me," Rachel said softly.

"Yes." Atticus put his hand lightly on her back, steering her down a hallway toward the restaurant where the brunch was being hosted. The restaurant was full, with a crowd waiting at the door, but Atticus gave his name and they were seated almost right away.

Rachel glanced around the dining room which was festively decorated with lots of greenery and red velvet bows. A Christmas tree was in one corner and a tall gold chair in another. High school girls in elf costumes were standing near the chair. "Where's Santa?" she asked.

"It looks like he's making the rounds. I see him over there right now," Atticus answered, gesturing to the opposite side of the room.

Sure enough, a portly, pink cheeked, white bearded Santa Claus was visiting with children at a table in the corner. His suit wasn't the cheap variety, either, but plush red with a luxurious white trim.

"He looks like the real thing," she said, spreading her napkin across her lap.

"Maybe he is."

She laughed and Atticus looked at her with a lifted eyebrow. "You don't believe?"

"You're talking to Rachel Mills," she answered. "I haven't believed since I was in second grade when I discovered a closet full of unwrapped presents, and then half of those presents ended up in my stocking, with the other half wrapped from Mom and Dad under the tree."

"You shouldn't have snooped."

"No," she agreed regretfully. "I grew up too fast, and I can't even blame Mom's cancer, but rather my determination to know 'facts.' My need for facts meant I had no patience for magic, fiction, or fantasy."

"I'm just the opposite. I wanted to believe in Santa Claus for as long as I could, and my parents encouraged me by letting me know that Santa only brought presents to the children that still believed, so I believed all the way through high school."

She laughed, vastly entertained by the idea of a muscular teenage Atticus opening his stocking on Christmas morning. "What were you getting in your high school stocking?"

"Oranges, chocolate, boxers, breath mints." He shrugged. "It wasn't about what was in the stocking. The fun was just having a stocking—" He broke off, his attention drawn to an elderly man trying to navigate the crowded room pushing his wife's wheelchair. A hostess was walking far in front of the couple, unaware that the couple was struggling. "Excuse me," he said, rising.

Rachel watched Atticus approach the couple and then begin moving people and their chairs so the husband could get his wife's wheelchair to their table.

Rachel's chest tightened and a tender lump filled her

throat. Atticus wasn't just kind to her. He was a kind human being, period.

Handsome, chivalrous, kind. He was someone she could lose her heart to. He'd turn her life inside out if she allowed it.

Did she want her life turned inside out?

Did she want that kind of change?

Atticus remained with the couple until they were settled at their table, and then returned to her. "Sorry about that," he said, sitting down again. "I saw them struggling and the hostess was oblivious."

"The hostess is young."

"She should have seated them at a table easier to reach. That was a nightmare."

"I'm glad you could help." She nodded to the waiter who'd come to fill their coffee cups. "I confess I didn't even notice them. I feel bad now."

"I'm just sensitive to the situation. My grandmother's been in a wheelchair for the past twenty-five years, and my grandfather tries hard to take care of her, but he's getting older, too. Makes me glad Holden is close."

"You don't think you'll ever live on the island?"

"Not cut out for island life. Love visiting, love the holidays and traditions, but it's not home."

"So Houston is most definitely home."

"I wouldn't say that, either. Home is where I'll raise my family." He hesitated. "Home would be a place a lot like

Marietta. I don't want to raise my kids in a big city, or the suburbs."

His words evoked a longing in her she couldn't decipher. He made family sound like something wonderful, and warm. "The winters are really long here."

"But there's so much to do in winter. Skiing, sledding, skating. I'd keep my kids busy with lots of activities."

"You ski?"

"I do okay."

"Which means you're probably an amazing skier. Most people who are modest about something tend to be extraordinarily talented."

"Do you ski?"

"I skied a little, when I was young. My mom and dad used to ski when they were first married, and I think they took me a couple times."

"So your dad doesn't ski anymore?"

"No, he worked a lot, and he's retired now, and I don't really know what he does to fill his time."

"You don't talk about him very much. Are you on bad terms?"

"Oh, no, we get along. In fact, I've been told I'm a lot like him. My mom was the touchy-feely one in the family. Dad's more contained."

"I think you're more touchy-feely than you want to admit."

"Yeah?"

"Yeah," he answered, smiling at her.

Her pulse did a jagged little jump. His smile was so beautiful.

"One day you'll have that husband and house and probably two or three kids running around, screaming at the top of their lungs," he added. "It will be absolute chaos, and pure joy."

She pretended to shudder. "That sounds terrifying."

"Control is overrated."

"Says the man who is always supremely in control?"

His smile turned cool and self-mocking. "If only that was true. I've made more mistakes, and bigger mistakes, than anyone else I know. I just don't let it stop—" He broke off, brow creasing, mouth compressing.

"You don't what?" she prompted gently, aware that his mood had changed very quickly, very dramatically.

He didn't immediately respond, and when he did, he sounded grim. "Years ago, I left a law practice I loved because I failed my client. I was too confident, and certain we had all the facts. The prosecutors annihilated the case, and my client went to jail. Had my client made mistakes? Yes. But his biggest crime was being in the wrong place, at the wrong time."

"What could you have done differently?"

"All of it. There should have been a better investigation. More research during the pretrial phase. I should have worked harder on a plea deal and settled out of court."

"So no more litigation for you."

"Nope."

"Do you miss it?"

"No. I was obsessive about my work. I didn't have much of a personal life."

"I can relate to that."

He smiled faintly. "When I was younger I had this idea of who I was going to be, and what I was going to do, and then things went sideways and I gave up the things I wanted, believing I didn't deserve them, as I'd just mess it all up." His lips quirked and his expression turned wry. "With time, I've forgiven myself for not being perfect and decided I still have the right to be happy, and have what I always wanted, which is a family of my own."

"You've been blessed with a close family."

"I have. They've been very supportive and it's taken me a while but I'm ready for more. I've been single. I've enjoyed my bachelor days. But I'm older and ready to settle down."

She was silent, processing everything he'd said, and he'd said a great deal. She'd learned more about him today during brunch than she had in the whole last week. "You were going to say something, though," she said, tracing their conversation back to the point where he stopped himself. "You were going to say you didn't let your mistakes stop you, or something like that."

He looked at her for a long moment. "I have avoided women like you. I have deliberately dated women that I couldn't see a future with, women who were 'fun for now,' rather than 'perfect for forever.'"

She blushed, suddenly feeling shy. "I didn't know there was such a category."

"It's not a spreadsheet kind of thing."

"Ah."

"You make me want all the things I've never had—the snug little Victorian on Bramble, the family, the traditions."

Her cheeks still felt hot but now her mouth had gone dry. She didn't know what to say. On one hand, his words filled her with fizzy emotion, making her feel like a bottle of champagne. On the other hand, none of his dreams meshed with her goals. And yet she was impossibly drawn to him. She loved looking at him. Loved everything about his face from the creases at his eyes, to the brackets at his mouth, and the warmth in his blue eyes. She'd come to Marietta for an old bookstore and had instead fallen in love with the most handsome, dashing, man she'd ever seen.

But how impractical this all was.

How impossible.

He was in Houston, she was in Irvine… and he talked of a home in Marietta.

She liked Marietta but couldn't imagine living here full-time. She couldn't imagine leaving her life in Irvine behind for the old bookstore, either.

None of this made sense. She was asking for pain and disappointment.

ATTICUS HEARD HER heavy sigh and glanced at her as he signed the check to his room, but her expression was shuttered, and she suddenly seemed distant.

They left the restaurant, and walking through the lobby, stopped to have a look at all the gingerbread houses from the competition yesterday. There were little houses and big houses, log cabins, Bramble House B&B, and even a replica of the Graff Hotel.

They made small talk as they admired the display and then stepped outside for the walk back to the bookstore.

Rachel buried her hands in her coat pockets. "Why have you never shown me your plans for the bookstore?" she asked.

He frowned but didn't immediately answer and Rachel pressed on. "Cormac Sheenan told me last night when he came by during the stroll that you'd had plans drawn up for your restaurant, and that they were pretty remarkable." She hesitated. "I'd like to see them."

"I don't think you're the ideal audience, Rachel."

"Why not?"

"You know why not."

Her forehead creased. "No, I don't."

"You do. We talked about the two dogs, one bone—"

"Oh, that."

"Yes, that," he said firmly.

She tipped her head back to look up at him. "But what if

I shouldn't have the bone?"

He frowned, uncertain where this was going. "You love the store."

"I wouldn't say I *love* it. I find it intriguing, it's a puzzle, and I'm starting to love some of the books, but I have a real job, and it's not here."

"You've given up on Paradise Books?"

"No. I started uploading books to a big online retailer today that specializes in old books."

"Good."

"But, come on, who is going to manage things when I'm not here? Who will input the thousands of books that fill the store? Who will mail the books out, and keep entries updated? The bookstore has so much potential, but only if someone really works hard at it. I don't know that I'm that person."

"Did Cormac put this idea in your head?" he asked, troubled.

"No. I'm just… worried. I have to go back one day—"

"Do you? You couldn't stay here? Find work here?"

"I'm an accountant, not a bookseller."

"So be an accountant, and hire someone to work the bookstore."

"Are you no longer interested in purchasing it?" she asked.

"Not if it's going to hurt us."

He saw her flinch at his words, and it caught him off

guard.

"You told me you've been trying to get Lesley to sell the store to you for the past eighteen months," she added flatly.

"Yes."

"But you're giving up on your dream, just like that?"

"Dreams can change."

"Not that quickly."

"There are other ways to do this."

"I want to see your plans, the ones Cormac mentioned."

He battled to hang on to his temper. Why was she so determined to be negative? She had options, so many options, and she refused to consider them. "Why?"

"Because I want to see how you'd use the building. I want to know how you'd reenvision the store."

"The books would be gone. The shelves would be gone. Only the brick, the crown molding, and the windows would remain," he said, tone curt. "Is that what you wanted to hear?"

"Where would the books go?"

"I don't know. It wasn't my problem," he answered. "I figured the books could be moved, someone could take one of those little houses on Church and turn it into a charming bookstore. Many of the houses have already been zoned for commercial use."

"That could still happen," she said. "Paradise Books wouldn't have to be closed. It would just be relocated. It'd also be a lot more affordable to run—smaller space, lower ceilings, all one floor."

"You'd need two houses then for all those books. You'd have to cut your stock in half."

"Which could work, if the online business picked up." She chewed her lip. "It's not a bad idea, you know. It could work if someone wanted to save the books."

"Rachel, *you* want to save the books."

"Do I?" She stopped walking and he was forced to stop, too. "Or is that what *you* think I should do?"

"Why don't we do this together? Why don't—"

"So, you're withdrawing your offer for the bookstore?" she interrupted, her voice short, clipped.

He sighed, arms folding over his broad chest. "Not officially, no. But I got a tip that the Bank of Marietta, across the street from the bookstore, might be closing its location, and opening a small branch in the new development north of here. It's also a landmark building, on a corner, with a lot of space."

"It doesn't have the brick you wanted, or the character."

"No. It has marble and high ceilings and fancy columns."

"That wasn't your vision for your Montana restaurant."

He shrugged. "Maybe I'm excited about what you can do with the bookstore. Maybe I realized those books are part of that historic building. The books are the heart of the building. How do I just dismantle that?"

"You have wanted Paradise Books for eighteen months, and now just a week after meeting me, you're giving up the dream. That's crazy, and wrong."

"What's crazy was me thinking only one place would do. I could put my next Galveston anywhere—Bozeman, Missoula, Big Fork. It doesn't even have to be in Montana. There's Wyoming, there's Idaho."

"You love Marietta."

His jaw hardened. "I'm not going to fight you for it anymore."

"So, your offer is off the table."

"You can make the bookstore work," he said. "If anyone could make it work, it's you."

"You're making me want to cry, and I never cry," she whispered, throat aching with emotion.

"You can do this, Rachel. *We* can do this, Rachel. Let's team up together—"

"*No.*"

"Why not?"

"Because we're not together, and we can't commit to big things together."

"I have a good gut."

"Not in this case. I'm sorry."

"*Rachel.*"

"I can't listen to this, and Atticus, you shouldn't want this. You've invested in plans. You have an architect and a contractor ready to go. I had no idea how much money you'd already poured into this—"

"Cormac had no business telling you any of that."

"This isn't about him, though. Don't be upset with him. This is about your goals, and mine, and they're not in sync. *We're* not in sync. I like you, I do, but you have no idea how much I regret coming to Montana right now. I came here on a lark and now neither of us will have what we wanted. It wasn't supposed to go this way."

"Nothing has changed."

RACHEL DREW A tremulous breath, and then another. She was angry, so angry. He'd changed everything because he'd changed.

He wanted more from her, but she didn't have more to give.

She'd enjoyed his attention, and had reveled in the romance, but that was all this was… a romance. It was fantasy. Nothing about this town or her time with Atticus had anything to do with her reality. "I'm not who you want, Atticus. I'm not who you need me to be."

"I don't need you to be anything but who you are—"

"This is so awkward, so uncomfortable. I hate that it's now uncomfortable."

He caught her chin and turned her face toward him. "I have fallen for you, Rachel. It wasn't part of my plan, but here we are, and I want to see you succeed. I want your Paradise Books to be the store it could be."

"And what if I don't want it—any of this? What if nothing in Marietta is right for me?"

He looked stunned for a moment and then his hand fell away. "Does that include me?" he asked stiffly.

She hated to hurt him, she did, but she had to be honest. "I'm sorry, Atticus, but we're not on the same page."

His dark head inclined. "Wow. Okay then. Good to know."

"So the bookstore—"

"I don't feel like discussing the store anymore." He glanced at the big brick building and then back at her. "You're going to do what you want to do, but it looks like it won't include me."

Chapter Nine

Upstairs in the attic apartment, Rachel numbly changed into sweatpants and a soft sweatshirt, doing her best to not think, feeling too confused to think.

She made a cup of tea, and sat facing the window on the foot of her bed, staring out at the jagged mountains. She felt trapped, and sad, disappointed in herself, but also disappointed in Atticus. Why did he have to ruin everything? Why couldn't things have continued as they were—sweet, lighthearted, fun?

Talking about marriage and children wasn't fun.

Talking about settling down wasn't fun.

Talking about building a business together wasn't fun.

She didn't need the complications and she didn't need the confusion. Things were already so hard and he'd made it all worse.

There was no way she could stay here now. There was no way she could open the bookstore tomorrow and pretend that everything was fine. Nothing was fine. She wasn't fine. And she was an idiot for thinking she could make a bookstore—*a bookstore*—work.

And yet Atticus…

He was just so much. He was too much… too much handsome, too much wisdom, too much wonderful. He made her feel like a juvenile wreck in comparison.

Her phone pinged with an incoming text.

She leaned across her bed and picked it up from the tiny nightstand. The message was from Atticus. *"Let's talk tomorrow."*

Blinking back tears, she deleted the text, and then immediately regretted it, and then kicked herself for regretting being strong.

She had to be strong now. She had to pull herself together. Everything here, including Atticus, was too much. She needed to go home to the place where everything made sense.

Atticus could have the bookstore. He could give the books to his mother. Rachel didn't care. She just wanted her life back, the one she understood, the one that felt safe, and familiar. Retrieving her laptop from the kitchen table, she bought her one-way ticket back home.

ATTICUS DIDN'T SLEEP well that night aware that the conversation with Rachel had gone badly. He kept checking his phone, hoping she'd reply. She didn't. He told himself to give her time. He knew he could be intense and overwhelming.

He hadn't thought she'd react quite so badly though. He'd even imagined she'd be glad—relieved—that he wasn't pushing for the store anymore. It wasn't as if she couldn't sell Paradise Books down the road, but after all she'd done this past week, why should she be in a hurry to get rid of it?

It didn't make sense.

But the way she'd looked at him when she'd said good night didn't make sense, either. The smile was gone. There was no light in her eyes. She looked shuttered. Detached. And that worried him.

Atticus went downstairs for breakfast and was on the way back to his suite when the man working the front desk flagged him down. "An item was left for you, Mr. Bowen. Let me get it from the back."

He returned a moment later with a book. "There's a letter, too, and I tucked it inside the cover," the clerk said. "The book and letter were dropped off early this morning."

Atticus took the book and turned it over and his chest tightened as he read the title on the worn dust jacket, *To Kill a Mockingbird.*

He knew immediately who'd left the book but waited until he was in the elevator on the way to his room to open the letter.

Atticus,

I thought your mom might like this for Christmas. I believe it's a first edition, but an 8th printing, so not the most valuable of first editions.

Thank you for your kindness and friendship, as well as your support. It meant a great deal to me.

I'm heading back to California now. If you want the bookstore, we can work out the details after the holidays. If you don't, perhaps you can pass the key to a reputable commercial Realtor and the Realtor can help me with the next steps.

All best, and happiest of holidays,
Rachel

Southern California was in the middle of a heat wave when Rachel arrived back in Orange County Monday afternoon. She peeled off her sweater as she retrieved her suitcase and waited for her ride, amazed at the difference between frigid Montana and blistering California. Standing at the curb with her suitcase she felt her phone vibrate. She glanced at her messages, expecting a text from Atticus.

Instead it was a message from her father, checking in with her.

She sent him a text that she was back and on her way to her place. She'd just hit send when her phone rang from an Orange County area code but she didn't recognize the number and let it go to voice mail. She played the voice mail once she could. It was Jared Helm calling, her immediate supervisor at Novak & Bartley. She was being offered the promotion.

She replayed Jared's message a second time.

Jay Shields had been fired—Jared didn't say why—but Jay was gone and the firm was offering her the promotion, if she wanted it.

If she wanted it.

Rachel hung up and clutched the phone in her fist. Why wouldn't she want it? This was what she'd worked so hard for. This was why she'd sacrificed so much. Of course she wanted it.

Part of her felt vindicated. Jay had not deserved the promotion. He'd barely pulled his weight. But now they were offering her the title, the raise, the recognition she'd craved.

And they'd offered her the promotion before she returned. They'd think she was coming back early from her holiday because of the raise, instead of her returning because she'd fallen in love, and that was beyond terrifying because falling in love would require change, and risk, and pain.

Falling in love meant she could lose Atticus. He could walk away from her at any point, or he could get sick and die. Far safer to not love, and not be hurt. Far safer to be obsessive about work rather than a person.

So she didn't have Atticus, but she had the promotion. She didn't have love, but she would soon earn substantially more money.

That was something, wasn't it?

RACHEL HAD NEVER found it hard to concentrate before, but

since returning from Marietta, her attention wandered constantly.

She was struggling being in the office, struggling at her computer, struggling to stay focused during meetings.

Fortunately, no one knew her well enough to know she wasn't on her game. Fortunately, she could hide her exhaustion behind her calm, professional mask.

But she hated the mask. It was just that—a fake persona she'd created so people would respect her, and not know how sensitive she really was.

She didn't let herself think about Atticus, though. And she didn't let herself think about Marietta or the bookstore, either.

She did find herself returning to her last morning there, and how she hadn't said goodbye to anyone when she left. She'd simply tidied up the store, emptied the refrigerator of perishables, unplugged the lights on the Christmas tree and yes, she'd agonized over the note she would be leaving for Atticus, because she didn't know how to say goodbye to him.

It was unthinkable that she was saying goodbye, but it was also unthinkable remaining, and feeling such strong feelings. She liked him far too much. She was becoming dependent on him and that wasn't healthy. And so, she'd stood, pen in hand, for the longest time, staring out at the sea of books, and remembered the moment he'd entered the store and introduced himself, extending a hand to her.

"Atticus Bowen," he'd said.

"Atticus?" she'd answered.

"My mother loved To Kill a Mockingbird.*"*

Rachel had raced upstairs and searched the *L* section and there she'd found a lone copy of *To Kill a Mockingbird*, and inside a tiny slip of paper read, *first edition, 8th printing, average wear and tear.*

Rachel hoped the book would be a suitable parting gift, and maybe it'd help smooth things over. After dropping the book and letter off at the hotel, Rachel drove her rental to Bozeman never intending to return to Montana again.

She'd done the right thing, she told herself, as she dragged herself into her second week back at the accounting firm. She'd worked too hard for too many years to not return. She'd earned the promotion. She *deserved* it.

And yet part of her felt lost. Part of her felt horribly empty.

Didn't she also deserve happiness?

But it seemed her vision for her life didn't have room for both. Or maybe she'd thought her goals would fulfill, making her happy.

She stared blindly at her computer screen, not seeing the spreadsheet, but Atticus.

She remembered how he'd wander into her bookstore in the mornings with a cup of coffee and his crooked, sexy smile.

She remembered his confidence and the way he'd look at her, eyebrow arched, blue eyes warm, silently challenging her. He'd loved to provoke her, and she'd secretly adored it. No one had ever looked at her that way, or teased her, or made her feel so important and so alive.

Shaking her head she reached up and brushed the dampness from her lashes. She had to stop this. It was time to settle and move on.

But she would miss him. She'd miss him terribly.

THANKFULLY THE SECOND week back was busy, with everyone preparing for the holidays and Novak & Bartley's Holiday Classic on Saturday, which featured a day of golf with key clients, followed by a VIP client dinner. All the other managers and directors attending were bringing dates to the dinner, but Rachel RSVPed just for herself.

It crossed her mind after she sent off the email that Atticus would have been a perfect date, but she'd burned bridges with him. Remembering that last conversation with Atticus made her cringe. She'd been so silly, and so dramatic, and ten days later it was still embarrassing to think about.

So she wouldn't think about it. She'd think about the tournament on Saturday and what she'd wear to the dinner Saturday night. This was one of the events she'd always wanted to attend and now she was. There was no room for regrets. She was accomplishing her goals, and doing the things she'd dreamed about.

THE GOLF TOURNAMENT was fine. She played fine. At least she hadn't been a disaster. She hadn't gotten drunk—like some of the managers and directors. She hadn't held the game up too much. She hadn't been too friendly or too formal. She'd held her own. And she was glad she played, even if it was a little bit of a letdown. She'd imagined golfing with the VIPs would have been somewhat more... fun. She'd imagined more camaraderie, or pleasure, or something. Instead, it'd been almost like work...

Well, worse than work. At least when she was working she wasn't obligated to maintain a conversation for four hours. That had been an eye opener.

The dinner dance in the clubhouse was somewhat better. She'd always been curious about the semiformal event, and it was pretty, the food was good, the band played their cover hits well. Again, conversation wasn't exactly scintillating, but she'd been polite and pleasant and stayed on until halfway through the dancing, sneaking out only when some of the clients began to leave, using their exit to make her own.

Monday at the office was quiet as most of the senior managers and directors had already begun their holidays with their families. A number had gone to Hawaii, while others were traveling to Vail or Jackson Hole.

The talk in the office about a white Christmas made her anxious. Her chest kept squeezing tight, and the air constricted in her throat, and she sat at her desk dizzy and lightheaded. She looked up the symptoms on the internet. No, that wasn't right. She wasn't having a panic attack. She hadn't had one of those since, well, her mom had died and her dad forced her to go to counseling because he was concerned about her grades and listless attitude.

But why would she be having a panic attack now?

She should be happy. She'd gotten what she wanted. The promotion, the raise, the invitation to golf and party with the senior team.

She had everything, didn't she?

And that was when her heart would pound too fast, and she'd get that dizzy, I'm-going-to-faint feeling again.

She didn't want to even consider she'd made a mistake leaving Marietta… and Atticus. But whenever she turned on the TV there was another Hallmark movie about snow and falling in love in an adorable snow-dusted small town.

But small towns weren't necessarily adorable. Small towns were a place where people knew her—and knew maybe too much about her. It was a place where she couldn't be invisible for long. She remembered her dismal open house, but then she remembered how everyone rallied to support her the next night, during the stroll. She'd been overwhelmed by the gifts and support, but at the same time, it had also been nice to feel like she belonged somewhere. Even with her recent promotion she didn't feel like she belonged at Novak & Bartley. She'd worked at the company for eight years, and yet just last week someone—admittedly a new person—asked if she was a temp.

Thinking of Marietta, she thought of all the things happening there. With Christmas approaching it must be fun. She found herself longing for fun.

Monday afternoon, Alicia said goodbye to Rachel as she was flying to Vancouver with her boyfriend who she was hoping planned to propose during their ski trip to Whistler.

Rachel wished Alicia a happy holiday and told herself not to be envious. Rachel had had the opportunity for more but she'd turned her back on romance.

But driving home, Rachel tapped her steering wheel restlessly, trying to distract herself from thinking of Atticus and Montana.

When she was little, she'd gone to Montana for Christmas a few times, driving to see her mother's family in Hamilton, nestled in the famed Bitterroot Valley. Rachel didn't remember much of those trips other than the drive was long.

Rachel wished she remembered more. She wished she hadn't tried so hard to block out memories of her mom. She wished she'd insisted she and her dad had kept up the family traditions after Mom had died.

What had some of those traditions been?

Definitely a tree, and the boxes of decorations that would come out each year—the white felt snowman wreath for the front door, the quilted stockings for the mantel, crimson candles, and a pair of angels singing.

Where were the angels? Were they in the boxes buried in

the attic?

Impulsively she called her father. "Dad, why did we stop decorating for Christmas?" she blurted when he answered.

"What?"

"We stopped putting up the Christmas tree and decorations. Why?"

"I think we agreed that first year we weren't in the holiday mood."

"And yet we put them up when Mom was alive going through chemo."

"She liked to lie on the couch, near the tree. It made her feel good."

"So we did it for her," Rachel said.

"Yes."

She felt a painful ache in her chest. "I liked the tree, too. And the angels."

"You and I talked about it and we thought it wasn't practical to do all that without your mom. She really was the spirit of Christmas."

And then she was gone.

Rachel's eyes burned and she swallowed around the lump filling her throat. Silence stretched across the line.

Her father cleared his throat. "I just didn't enjoy any of it without her," he said. "And you said you didn't, either."

"Dad, I was just seventeen when she died."

"We had to make some changes," he said.

"But maybe we shouldn't have stopped doing everything.

Maybe we should have done it in her memory? You know, tried to keep her memory alive?"

He sighed. "But you were so devastated by her death. Two years of counseling—"

"She was my mom."

"You didn't need to be constantly reminded of what you'd lost. I was trying to protect you, trying to help you move forward. You didn't want to be going to therapy forever."

Rachel felt something wet on her cheek and brushed it away. A tear. And another. "I probably should have continued the therapy." Her voice was husky. "Because I haven't been living, Dad—"

"You're just tired, Rachel," he said patiently. "You work hard. You always work so hard."

"I think I work hard because I'm not happy."

"You work hard because you enjoy being successful."

"I'm lonely."

"There have been plenty of smart, successful men interested in you. Greg, for example. I liked him."

"He was boring."

"You're a little bit boring."

"Dad."

"I'm just saying you don't have to be alone. It's your choice."

She couldn't argue with him on that. "So what are you doing for Christmas? Are we getting together? Doing Chinese again?"

He hesitated. "I've been invited to Palm Desert by a friend of mine. Would you mind if I went?"

"Not at all, Dad. That sounds like fun." And then she added, "Is it a woman friend? Possibly a girlfriend?"

"I'm too old to have a girlfriend. She is a lady friend."

Rachel smiled crookedly. "Good for you, Dad."

"You don't mind?"

"*No.* Just because I'm alone doesn't mean you should be."

"Rachel?"

"Yes, Dad?"

"Would you like your mother's angels?"

Her eyes prickled and burned all over again. For a moment she couldn't speak. "Yes, I would."

At home, Rachel dug through her closet, moving shoe boxes and suitcases to find the bulletin board she'd pinned all her hopes and dreams on back when she was a college coed, and carried the board to her bed, where she propped it up against the pale blue pillows.

The vision board looked a lot like her desk drawer—orderly, clean, beautifully organized with everything in its place. Her goals were typed, listed in numeric form. Goals were very specific, too—her desired income, retirement nest egg, means to achieving financial stability, promotions. The sole visual on her board was the photo of a smiling blonde woman in a nice gray suit standing in the middle of a large, glossy office. And that was Rachel's vision for her life, and her future. A single woman in a suit, standing alone in a big, impersonal, but luxurious, office.

Rachel exhaled and sat down on the foot of the bed, wondering at the girl who'd thought this was the picture of success.

But then, the girl who made this was the one who'd gone through years of grieving for a mother who'd died too young. That girl was afraid of emotions, afraid of attachment. That girl just wanted security, and control.

Rachel read through the goals and they were all very impressive, but there was no room for friends, no room for a boyfriend, no room to fall in love. How could she ever fall in love when love would break her heart? How could she want a family when someone might die?

She could hear Atticus's voice in her head. *Change happens with or without your approval. That's just life.*

Being alone wasn't going to protect her. Keeping everyone at arm's length wouldn't save her. She was going to have to take risks and live.

She thought of Atticus and her heart ached. Was he back in Houston, or had he gone to Galveston to join his family? She envied his family and friends for still having him. She'd given him up rather than adjust her goals. So stupid. Rachel despised herself for being a coward. At the rate she was going, she would die alone, surrounded by very nice things.

Horrendous.

She looked at her vision board and exhaled hard. Was this really what she wanted for herself? Things, not people? Work, not love? What a lonely future. What a bleak life it would be.

Fighting tears, she jumped up and tore the advertisement of the woman in the glossy office off the bulletin board, and then she ripped the list of goals down next and shredded it into a dozen pieces. She kept ripping it apart until it was just a bare corkboard and then she cried, tears she never cried, tears for the girl who missed her mother terribly, and felt so much guilt for not being stronger for her mother when her mother needed her. She cried for the girl who believed that numbers would somehow protect her.

Numbers couldn't protect her from disappointment. Being defensive was stunting her. She needed to be proactive. She needed a new dream.

The ringing of her doorbell forced her to scrub her face dry and pull herself together. Opening the door, she discovered her father on her doorstep with two medium cardboard boxes.

"It's Christmas Eve tomorrow. I thought maybe we could put the angels out tonight."

For a moment she was speechless, and then she hugged her dad tightly, emotion making it impossible to speak.

Together they unwrapped the angels, and Rachel lightly touching one of the angels' sweet face, before placing the pair in the middle of her dining table, a table she'd never once used since she didn't entertain and usually ate at her desk or on the couch. Then she unpacked the rest of the boxes, discovering two cartons of glass ornaments, a handful of ornaments made by Rachel as a little girl in Girl Scouts. There were a half-dozen Christmas records, and two books.

She reached for the book with the brilliant crimson cover, *The Life and Adventures of Santa Claus* by L. Frank Baum, and opened it. The book had been inscribed,

To Dottie & Bessie
Merry Christmas
From the Sondersons
1919

Dottie and Bessie. She recognized those names. There had been a whole box of books with those names in the back room of Paradise Books.

"Dad, who was Dottie and Bessie?" she asked, looking up at her father. "Why would Mom have this book?"

He leaned over her shoulder to read the elegant penmanship. "If I'm remembering correctly, Bessie was the nickname for your mother's grandmother, Elizabeth. Dottie was her sister. I knew Grandmother Elizabeth, but I never met her great-aunt, Dottie. She'd passed away a number of years before I met Mom."

"Where did they live?"

"Montana. They moved around a bit as their father worked for the railroad."

Rachel reached for the other children's book. *The Secret Garden*, and this one had Bessie in it, too, and Rachel flashed back to the books she'd catalogued in Marietta, the set of *Five Little Peppers*, *The Red Cross Girls*, along with the well-loved edition of *Little Men*.

Bessie. Elizabeth.

All those boxes of books in the backroom at Paradise Books, boxes of books that hadn't been shelved.

"I need to call Lesley," she said.

Her father frowned. "Why?"

"I have questions."

"I thought you'd decided to sell the store."

"But it hasn't sold, and it's still mine, and there are things I want to know."

"You got the promotion you wanted, Rachel."

"I know, but what if this isn't right for me? What if it's time to do something else?"

"All you've wanted for the past ten years is security."

"But maybe I'm going about it all wrong. Maybe my dream is changing." She saw from his expression that he didn't understand. "I set all these goals when I was young, and grieving, and afraid to be hurt. I created goals that kept people out. I'm not that same girl anymore. I'm ready to take chance. Ready to let people in."

"That makes sense," he said gruffly. "Just be careful though. You don't want to throw away everything you've worked for."

She gave him a hug. "That won't happen, Dad," she whispered against his shoulder. "I'm too practical."

After her dad left Rachel calculated the time in Queensland. Eight o'clock Monday night was one o'clock Tuesday for Lesley, which meant it was already Christmas Eve for Lesley.

Rachel didn't leave a message the first time she called, but when she phoned back an hour later, she again got Lesley's cheery voice saying she wasn't available but please leave a message and she'd return the call.

Merry Christmas, Lesley, it's Rachel Mills, your goddaughter. I'd love to talk to you about the bookstore, and some of the books I've found.

She waited another hour, and then phoned again. *Lesley, it's Rachel again. I'm not sure if you're home for the holidays or with your sister, but I'd love to talk to you about the bookstore, and something I found in my mom's things. Could you please call me back? You can call me collect, anytime, too.*

Lesley never called, and Rachel went to bed troubled. When she woke up, she sipped her coffee and looked at the angels sitting on the dining room and wondered if Lesley was okay. Had something happened to her?

Rachel gathered her courage and texted Atticus. *"I've been calling Lesley and leaving messages. Do you know if she's okay?"*

He answered twenty minutes later. *"Are you calling her landline? That might be why she'd not answering. Lesley and her family have arrived in Marietta for Christmas."*

Lesley was in Marietta?

And how did Atticus know that? Was he also in Montana? *"Are you in Marietta?"* She typed before she could change her mind.

"Just until the morning, and then it's home for Christmas."

And just like that, Rachel knew where she wanted to be.

Chapter Ten

THERE WERE NO cheap last-minute flights to Bozeman. In fact, there were almost no flights at all. Getting to Bozeman meant three connecting flights, with a long layover in Salt Lake City, but she didn't mind if it meant she could get in tonight because she was desperate to see Atticus before he left tomorrow.

It was seven o'clock now, and in Salt Lake for a two-hour layover, waiting for the third and final leg of her trip. The Bozeman flight was delayed due to a storm in Atlanta, but at least her flight was scheduled to still go out whereas others were being canceled right and left.

But as the evening wore on, and her flight continued to be pushed back, she tried to stay positive. As long as her flight wasn't canceled, she'd still get there. It didn't matter if she arrived midnight Christmas Eve, as long as she arrived. She was trying not to think about what she'd do if her flight was canceled because at this point it wasn't an option.

She'd debated all day whether she should let Atticus know she was coming. She didn't know why she was reluctant to tell him. Did she think just surprising him in the morning would make everything better?

She wasn't so sure.

Call him, she told herself. Let him know you're coming.

But she was afraid, unsure of his reaction.

Rachel tried not to panic as her connecting flight was pushed back yet another half hour, while new flights were now being canceled.

She found herself praying for her plane to arrive.

She prayed that Atticus would want to see her.

She prayed that—

Her prayer was interrupted by the ringing of her phone. She fished the phone out of her purse.

It was Atticus.

"Hello," she said answering.

"Just wanted to wish you a merry Christmas," he said.

Her chest grew tight, tender with bottled emotion. "Merry Christmas to you, too. How are you doing? What did you do tonight?"

"Had dinner with the Sheenans, and then went to the caroling service at St. James with Lesley and her family."

"Sounds like a wonderful Christmas Eve."

"It's been nice. But it'll be good to see my family tomorrow." He paused, cleared his throat. "What about you? How is your Christmas Eve?"

She glanced around the crowded airport with all the stressed and unhappy looking people. "Not as nice as yours."

"I hope you're not alone."

"Oh, no, definitely not alone."

"Good." He paused, and silence stretched. "I just wanted you to know I was thinking of you."

"I'm glad you called. I was thinking about you, too."

Another beat, one that made her heart ache.

"Merry Christmas, Rachel."

Tell him you're coming, tell him you're on the way, tell him not to leave before you get there. But the words stuck in her throat and her eyes had that terribly dry, gritty feeling and she was afraid of being hurt, and not being enough. She was trying to change but maybe it was too little, too late. "Merry Christmas, Atticus."

They hung up, and she squeezed her eyes closed, squeezed them painfully tight, but even then, it didn't hold back her tears.

She should have just told him. She should—

She reached for her phone and typed a quick message to Atticus. *"I'm sitting in the Salt Lake airport hoping my Bozeman flight will still leave tonight. Wanted to see you for Christmas, but if I don't make it before you go, know that I tried."*

She didn't have to wait long for a reply. *"I hope it works out. Keep me posted."*

RACHEL LANDED IN Bozeman at midnight, the plane taxiing down the runway in a swirl of falling snow.

But she'd arrived, and she'd only brought a carry-on bag with her which meant she could head straight out. Unfortunately, the rental car booths were closed, and there were no taxis in front of the terminal. Standing at the curb, she tried her ride share app, but nothing was available. It seemed as if everyone was already home, tucked in for the night. She didn't blame them. The snow was lovely but it was cold and she was exhausted and just wanted to be snug in a warm bed.

A big SUV pulled up in front of her and the passenger window rolled down. "Need a ride?" a very handsome man, wearing a fancy sheepskin coat, asked.

She didn't think she'd ever been so happy to see anyone before. "Yes. Thank you!"

He came around, gave her a swift hug before taking her bag and stowing it in the back.

He'd felt so good, so big, and so right that some of her anxiety melted. "What are you doing here?" she asked, as he opened the passenger door for her.

"Making sure I saw you before I left," he answered, closing the door behind her.

His answer made her heart ache. She'd only arrived. She wasn't ready to think of saying goodbye, and she wasn't going to focus on goodbyes. Not yet. "I'm grateful." She smiled at him, content to just drink him in. "You're looking well."

He flashed her a grin. "I had a haircut a few days ago."

She gurgled with laughter, and then it hit her that this was the first time she'd laughed since she'd left Marietta two weeks ago. "How did you know when I'd arrive?"

"Tracked your flight."

"Thank you for that."

He shot her a glance as he left the airport and turned on the frontage road. "So, what brings you to Marietta?"

"You. Lesley." She wrapped her hands around one knee and started out the windshield where the wipers were rhythmically swishing away snow. "The bookstore." He said nothing and she quietly added, "But mostly you."

She felt rather than saw him look at her. She kept her gaze fixed on the window and the small, lacey snowflakes.

"Things not going well back home?" he asked carefully.

"They're going according to the plan." She chewed on her lip, wondering how to tell him everything that had happened, and everything she'd learned. Maybe best to start small. "I got the promotion."

"You did?"

She nodded. "I got the call on the day I flew back into John Wayne Airport."

"Congratulations."

"Thank you." She waited another moment before adding, "I played in the holiday classic, it's Novak & Bartley's Christmas golf tournament for their big clients. I did okay considering it was the first time I've actually played with anyone other than my instructor."

"Good for you."

She heard the warmth in his voice and she looked at him in time to catch his smile. "I was so nervous."

"Was it fun?"

"Not really."

"Why not?"

"It was kind of boring actually."

He choked on smothered laughter. "You probably got a bad foursome."

"That's what I keep telling myself." She wrinkled her nose. "But maybe it's me. My dad said I'm boring."

He laughed out loud this time. "He said what?"

"That I'm boring."

"I would never, in a million years, describe you as boring. Now, I might call you stubborn, obstinate, inflexible—"

"I'd prefer tenacious and persistent."

Atticus smiled and shook his head, but he said nothing else and Rachel was content to sit, listening to the Christmas carols playing on the satellite radio station. Hard to believe she'd made it to Montana after all. It had been such a stressful day trying to get here. "What is Lesley like?" she asked. "You said you went to church with her tonight, so you must get along with her."

"She's exactly what you expect. Warm, kind, sweet, funny, helpful, determined to make everyone feel good."

"You didn't tell her I was planning on selling the bookstore, did you?"

"No."

"Did you tell her I was coming?"

"No."

Rachel fidgeted in her seat, suddenly uncomfortable. "Have you decided if you want to buy the bookstore?"

He glanced at her, expression sober. "Let's not do this now. You only just got here."

"But you're leaving in the morning."

"And sometimes less is more."

Prickly heat rushed through her, and she looked out the window, and blinked hard, horrified that she was going to cry now, in front of him, but she was tired, and overly emotional. She had to keep control or this entire trip would end in disaster.

ATTICUS SAW THE tears in her eyes and his gut cramped. The last thing he wanted was to make her cry.

He reached over and took her fist in his hand, his thumb stroking over her tightly clenched fingers. "That came out the wrong way. I'm sorry."

Her throat worked. She was still holding back the tears but she gave a faint nod.

"Did you want to see me because you wanted to see me? Or did you want to see me to talk about the bookstore?"

A tear fell, a glistening streak on her pale cheek. She reached up with her free hand to brush it away. "See you," she said brokenly.

His gut burned and his chest felt heavy. He gently worked her fist open, and laced his fingers through hers. "I'm going to be honest, and I hope this doesn't hurt you, but I'm not interested in the bookstore anymore, Rachel. I'm just interested in you."

She drew a raw breath. "I'm good with that."

"Yeah? Because sometimes everything is just business with you."

"I know, and I'm working on changing that." Her fingers tightened around his. "That's why I'm here. I wanted to see you. I needed to see you. You're the best part of my life and I'm here to figure out how to keep you in it—" She broke off, gulped for air. "Romantically. You make a great friend, but I'd like more with you, if you're open to that."

He lifted her hand to his mouth, and kissed the back of her hand. "Most definitely open to that."

"Really?"

He laughed at her astonished tone, and gave her an amused look. "I want it all with you. It's not a secret. We should be on the same team. I can see a future with you—marriage, children, our own Marietta home."

"Wow."

"Is that a good wow, or a bad wow?"

She laughed tremulously, and she gave his fingers another squeeze. "It's an I-can't-believe-this-is-happening wow." She turned in her seat, facing him. "I was so afraid I'd lost you. So afraid I'd missed my opportunity."

"I wasn't going anywhere, Rachel."

"But I rejected you. I ran away."

"I knew you'd come back."

"How?"

Fingers still laced together, he placed their joined hands on his thigh, just above his knee. "I just knew you. You were overwhelmed. But you're tough, and persistent, and you don't give up." He glanced at her. "And here you are."

FRESH TEARS SHIMMERED in her eyes. Her lower lip quivered before she ruthlessly bit into it. "You're making me cry."

"That's okay, as long as I can also make you smile and laugh."

"You do. You're the only one who can make me laugh."

"We'll have to broaden your circle of acquaintances then."

She laughed, and they drove the rest of the way to Marietta in silence, but the kind of silence where it felt warm and safe and unbearably good.

"Your apartment is ready for you," he said, as he turned off Highway 89. "Even managed to stick a few things in the fridge for you for the morning."

"How did you manage that on Christmas Eve?"

"I know people."

She grinned and looked out the window, excited to be back. Most of downtown Marietta was dark, with just the holiday lights shining on the turn-of-the-century-style streetlamps. But as they approached Paradise Books, her corner building glowed.

Rachel glanced at Atticus and then back to the bookstore. The window displays had been redone. She couldn't yet see the details but they were filled with rich jeweled color and sparkling lights.

Atticus parked his SUV in front of the store. She jumped out of her side and went up to the window facing Main. The scene was spectacular, a vision straight from the pages of *The Nutcracker*. Heavy red velvet curtains framed the large Plateglass windows, the fabric pulled back with golden tassels allowing the rich crimson to ripple and swag. A legion of nutcrackers fought a rat army, while a delicate ballerina pirouetted above. Different versions of the book balanced on glass snowflakes. It was gorgeous and magical.

"This is incredible," she exclaimed, as Atticus joined her at the window, her travel bag in his hand. "Who did it?"

"Sadie."

"It's amazing."

"She changed the windows out last weekend, too."

"Why?"

"She wanted people to pay attention, and it's worked. Even before Lesley arrived, the bookstore was starting to get foot traffic. You've sold quite a few books."

"*I* didn't sell them," she corrected. "So you're telling me the bookstore stayed open this entire time?"

"Yes. I ran things the first week, and then Lesley and her sister arrived last Sunday, and Lesley took over."

"She must think I'm awful."

"No, not at all. She knows you have a career in California, and she had a great time here. She was in her element. And you wouldn't believe the number of people who came to see her."

"I'm not surprised. Everyone loves her."

"People love the books, too. One person bought the entire Mark Twain series you had."

"I didn't know there was an entire Twain series here."

"He paid over six hundred and thirty-five dollars for the set. I probably could have gotten more, but I didn't want to jeopardize the sale."

"You did all this for me."

"I did it for us. I believe in us."

She didn't think she'd ever heard anything so lovely in her entire life. "I love the way you say 'us.'"

"You didn't a couple weeks ago."

"I was terrified."

He reached for her, and wrapped his arms around her, holding her close. "Not terrified anymore?"

"More terrified of missing out on the best thing I've ever known." She stood up on tiptoe to kiss him. "You're the best thing. You're kind of amazing."

"I know." And then he kissed her, and it was a kiss that went on and on, and by the time he was done, Rachel was warm and tingly from head to toe.

"Merry Christmas," she said, overwhelmed by the joy she

felt. Everything in her was full of hope and light.

"Merry Christmas, Rachel. So glad you came back." He unlocked the front door, flicked on the overhead light and handed her the key. "So what made you decide this is where you wanted to be?"

"Besides missing you?" she asked, stepping into the store.

He remained on the threshold. "Yes."

She gestured to the store, and then the street covered in white powdery snow. "I realized I didn't like my vision board. It wasn't... me. And when I pictured what I wanted, and what I needed, it wasn't the big office, or the large corporation. I need people, and love. I need you. I want to have what I lost when my mom died. Family. Traditions. Feelings." She laughed even as she blinked back tears. "This is crazy. I haven't cried in years, and now I can't stop! I have so many feelings and oh, Atticus, I think I love you."

"Good. Because I know I love you."

He closed the door behind her and kissed her, and the kiss made her knees weak and her head spin. Rachel clung to his thick jacket, thinking she had to be dreaming. She'd been so alone for so long, locked inside of herself, locked in with her grief and somehow her heart felt wide open, open to love, love to change, open to a future she hadn't even imagined could exist for her.

It was a miracle.

"Stay," she whispered.

"We won't get any sleep if I stay, and we're going to

need sleep if we're to be in good form for Lesley's tomorrow. We've been invited to Lesley's for Christmas morning and we can't not show."

"You're not leaving for Texas?"

"I'm going to catch a later flight."

"Will Lesley mind if I show up uninvited?"

"No. She, like me, was hoping you'd find your way back to Marietta for Christmas. It's one of the reasons Lesley came home."

Rachel's eyes filled with hot tears. "Everyone had such faith in me… faith I didn't even have."

"And yet you're here."

She felt like she'd swallowed the sun and moon and was full of light. But not just light. She felt a new calm, and strength. "Do you think my mom's here?" she whispered. "Because I think I feel her."

He wiped away one of her tears, and then another. "I wouldn't be surprised. Even though she's not physically here anymore, her spirit remains."

"You believe that?"

"I do, and I believe she'll always love you. Your mom wants you happy." He kissed her gently. "And I do, too. I'll be back tomorrow at ten. How does that sound?"

"Like I can sleep in."

"Do you really sleep in?"

She grinned and shook her head. "No."

"Didn't think so. Good night, Rachel."

"Good night, Atticus. Thank you for picking me up."
"Anytime. Every time."

RACHEL'S HEAD WAS still spinning as she climbed up the stairs to her apartment, stripped off her clothes and tumbled into her bed, which smelled sweet and fresh as if the sheets and pillowcases had just been washed.

She suspected someone had done that for her, too.

It was overwhelming because she wasn't used to people doing things for her. Ever since her mom got sick, Rachel had been the one to take charge, make plans, get things done. And now people, who were almost still strangers, were doing things for her.

It boggled her mind.

And yet it also felt incredibly good. To think she might actually be important to someone… to think she might *belong* somewhere…

Rachel fell asleep, humming with warmth, and brimming with gratitude.

LESLEY LIVED IN a big handsome house with tall white columns on Bramble, just a few blocks from Bramble House Bed and Breakfast, and Lesley was exactly as Rachel remembered—short, slightly round, with a sweet face, smiling eyes, and gray curly hair.

When she spotted Rachel behind Atticus, she gave her the biggest hug. "Oh, my goodness, what a gift this is. So very, very glad to have you with us this Christmas."

"I almost didn't make it," Rachel confessed, following Lesley into the house. "My flight was one of the few that got out last night."

"So glad you did. I was hoping to see you, and Atticus was so sure you'd come."

They both shot Atticus a glance, and he shrugged, smiled, and excused himself saying he needed to put the champagne in the refrigerator.

"I tried to call you," Rachel said. "I left a couple messages so don't be surprised when you get back to Australia. All is well, I just wanted to talk."

"And now you're here. What can I tell you?"

"This is probably not the best time. It's Christmas and you're making breakfast—"

"Everything is ready, and the casserole is in the oven. There is nothing to do, and since it is Christmas, I can't think of a better time to talk than now, can you?"

Lesley led the way into the living room beautifully decorated with a tall slender Christmas tree. "Come sit next to me," Lesley said, sitting down on the couch and patting the cushion next to her. "Tell me why you were calling. What happened? What did you need?"

"I don't even know. This gift of the bookstore has baffled me. I honestly didn't understand why you would give me something like this. I know nothing about books. I rarely read a book and the bookstore isn't even in Southern California but all the way here in Montana. In the beginning, I just didn't get it, but as I spent time in the store, and went through some of the boxes of books in the back room I began to fall in love with the books. I began to fall in love with the inscriptions. So many of the books had been given to someone for a birthday or Christmas. So many of the books were gifts from grandparents and parents and I found it really moving, and I'm not a touchy-feely kind of person. But it really made an impression on me that these books, seventy-five, one hundred, one hundred and twenty-five years old, all had mattered to someone. These books are well read, and loved, and as I added them to a database, I noticed certain names appeared over and over. Bessie… Dottie… Elizabeth."

Rachel drew a deep breath. "Monday after work, my dad brought over two Christmas boxes that had belonged to my mom, and in them were two more books, books inscribed to Bessie and Dottie." She looked up at Lesley. "My dad said my mother's grandmother was named Elizabeth, and when she was young she was called Bessie." She hesitated, searching for the right words. "Is it just a fluke, or are any of those books in the back room my mother's?"

"We're talking about the fourteen boxes in the back room," Lesley said.

Rachel nodded.

"The fourteen boxes of books that aren't on my shelves." Rachel nodded again.

"Those aren't actually your mother's books anymore, Rachel. Those are your books. I've been holding on to them ever since your mother went to college and didn't return. They were family books, books that, as you say, belonged to her grandmother, and her great-aunt, Dottie, as well as other members of the family. I offered to ship the books to California several times but your mother said there was no place to put them, and then I had the store, and she said I should sell them since there really was no reason to hang on to them, but as your godmother, I knew they were your legacy. They're a piece of your mother's past, and I've been keeping them for you."

"What if I didn't want them, or the bookstore?"

"Then you'd sell the store and move on with your life."

"You wouldn't have minded?"

"It was my gift to you. No strings attached."

"But you could have just sold the bookstore to Atticus. He wanted the store, and you would have made a lot of money."

Lesley shrugged. "Life isn't just about making money."

"Yes, but… you've given away something you've loved."

"To you, someone I love."

The lump was back in Rachel's throat. "You barely know me."

"But I knew your mother, and adored her, and you are

her only child."

Rachel clasped her hands tightly, fighting for control. "I wish my mom had talked more about growing up in Marietta. I wish she'd talked about *you*."

"Instead, she probably focused on you, and your studies, and your interests. That's what good moms do. They take care of their families." Lesley reached out and patted her cheek. "And your mother may not have talked about Montana and me, but she talked to me about you, and how proud she was of you, and of all the great things you were going to do with that brilliant brain of yours."

"Did she really say that?" Rachel whispered.

"She did. Every time we spoke, and every time we wrote. You took high school math courses in junior high, and college math classes in high school. You were captain of the math team at your school, and you tutored math and science in your free time to earn money." Lesley smiled. "Your mom was a smart, successful woman, but she always said you were her greatest accomplishment, and her biggest joy."

The tears Rachel had been fighting fell. "I miss her. So much."

Lesley covered Rachel's fists, holding them tight. "I know. She left us far too soon."

"She did," Rachel agreed.

"And the bookstore, you don't have to keep it. It's not meant to be a burden. If Atticus wants to turn it into a steak house and you're good with that, then do it."

"I don't think he wants it anymore."

"The point is, it's yours, and it's not meant to be a ball and chain. If you can sell it and do something good with the money, then fantastic. If you want to keep it, and reinvent the store in some way, I support that. I simply want you happy."

"Are you ever going to move back here?"

"That's a good question. I don't know. It feels really good to be back, but my sister has her kids and family in Queensland, and I like being surrounded by kids and young people." She glanced up as Atticus appeared in the doorway.

"A timer is going off," he said. "And your sister didn't know if the foil needed to come off the casserole or if it's ready to come out of the oven."

"Tell her I'm coming," Lesley said, before pushing a wave of Rachel's hair back from her cheek. "Life is short. There are no guarantees. Seize happiness, and don't let it go."

They lingered after the late breakfast, staying into early afternoon, before saying their goodbyes to Lesley and her sister, and began the walk back to downtown.

It was cold but clear, and everything sparkled from last night's snow. Atticus held her hand, keeping her close at his side, and Rachel enjoyed the brisk walk, relishing the fresh air and the exercise. As they traveled down Bramble they pointed out houses they liked, and which one they could see as a suitable first house. They played the game all the way until they reached Main Street, and as they turned the corner onto Main, Rachel felt a welling of appreciation. She'd been charmed from the start by the small town's historic Western facades, and mellow brick buildings, and she loved the way snowcapped Copper Mountain rose up behind the domed courthouse. But most of all, she loved the people who were raised here, and were drawn here, and chose to make a life here.

She wanted to make a life here, too.

"You really don't want the bookstore?" she asked as they crossed the street to Paradise Books.

"I'd have to pull out the books, and I don't want to do that."

"So it has to stay a bookstore."

"Don't you think it should?" he asked, looking down at her.

"What about your restaurant?"

"I'm in talks with the bank on the opposite corner. They are not yet ready to move, but when they are, they know I'm interested in their space."

"So I get my bookstore, but you're not sure if you get your restaurant."

"I'm not worried."

"But without a restaurant here, what will you do in Marietta?"

"The same thing I do in Houston. Return calls, answer emails, hold meetings, travel when needed." He kissed her, and then added in a low voice, "As well as do all the things I couldn't do in Houston… make love to you, kiss you senseless, fix up our house, explore the area, do ski trips… should I go on?"

"No. I'm still stuck on the making love part." Heat bloomed in her cheeks as she unlocked the front door and then swung the door open. "But we could also make things work if you need to be in Houston, closer to your family."

"That might be something for us to discuss one day, but I'd love to start our life together here. We met here."

"Found love here," she agreed shyly as he entered the store behind her, and closed the door. She wrapped her arms around him, and tilted her head back to see his face. "This has been the best Christmas ever—" And then she broke off, remembering he was supposed to leave. "What time is your flight? Don't you have to leave soon?"

"I ended up canceling my flight," he said, kissing her nose, and then her lips. "I called my parents this morning and explained that something had come up, but I'll definitely be back for New Year's. They host a big party at my grandparents in Galveston every year. It's quite the shindig."

"Were they upset that you canceled on them last minute?"

"No, because they knew I was hoping you'd show up."

"They know about me?"

"Of course. You're the girl I'm going to marry."

She grabbed the pockets of his coat and held on. "You

didn't say that."

"I did, and more."

"You're so sure of yourself," she said, "but I do like a man with confidence." And then she hesitated, a wobble in her voice. "So, when do you go to Houston?"

"Depends on when you can go. I'm planning on taking you home with me. I'd like to introduce you to my family. Maybe you'll go with me for New Year's?"

The idea was so incredibly tempting. "Won't they think we're moving too fast?"

He shook his head. "My mom and dad knew the moment they met that they were meant to be. They waited three months before they married, but that was a long engagement compared to my grandparents in Galveston. They eloped after just one week."

"You Bowen men move fast."

"We know a good thing when we see it." He drew back and peeled off his coat. "Speaking of good things, I have something for you." He led her toward the Christmas tree and kneeling down, he pulled out a long white tube from beneath the tree's thick branches.

"It was just an idea," he said. "You will probably have better ones."

She carried the tube back to the counter, and drew out the roll of white paper. They were architectural plans, she realized, as she unrolled the paper. Plans for the bookstore from the look of it. She glanced at Atticus but his expression betrayed nothing. He helped her flatten the plans, though, by placing a book on one side, while she used a paperweight to hold down the other.

"So, tell me what I'm looking at," she said, scanning the large rectangle with smaller black boxes and lines. "I see the front door, and the corner windows. I see the stairs, too, but what is all this?" she asked, gesturing to an area against the far wall, one that right now held nonfiction books, mostly travel and cookbooks and some self-help.

"That's your coffee bar," he said, leaning on his elbows and smiling at her.

"My coffee bar?"

"You'd really only need one, maybe two, baristas, and when it's slow they can help you with your online book business."

She arched a brow. "My online business."

"It's going to be profitable."

"And what is this area back here, in what is currently the big storage room? Please tell me it's not a kitchen."

"It's not. It's your new children's section, complete with a little stage for guest authors and story time." He tapped another square. "That's your elevator to the second floor, and this here is your fully accessible bathroom, so that everyone can use the facilities."

"You have thought of everything," she said, flipping the page over and studying the second page, and then realizing there was a third. "What is this? My little apartment?"

"Remember, it's just an idea," he said.

She frowned as she studied the plans. The kitchen/living room looked different, as did the bedroom. In fact, the bedroom was gone and the kitchen/living room looked considerably smaller. "What's happened to it?"

"It's an office, in case you wanted to have your own accounting business here. You already own the building. You've lost some of the kitchen because the elevator goes straight up to the third floor now, but you still have room for a small refrigerator, sink, and microwave. The living room is a meeting space, or reception space if you have clients coming, and the bedroom is now your office. You'll note that we have your desk facing the window so you can see Copper Mountain and the Gallatin Range."

She looked at him in wonder. "You've thought of everything."

"I wanted to give you reasons to stay."

Overwhelmed she reached out and put her hand on his chest just to feel the strong drumming of his heart. "You're my reason to stay," she said unsteadily. "You're all I need to stay."

"I know how important your work is to you—"

"I'll be fine workwise. I'm not worried. I'm not worried about anything."

He drew her even closer, his hands low on her hips. "Nothing?"

"For the first time in my life, I'm not worried. I have

such confidence about the future. But not just confidence, excitement. This is going to be fun. You and me, together. We're a team."

"And we're going to have an adventure."

"I'm ready."

"Me, too. Merry Christmas, Rachel."

"Merry Christmas, Atticus. May this be the first of many, many."

And then he kissed her, and there were no more words for a very long time.

Epilogue

They didn't rush into marriage, or an engagement, because Rachel—despite being madly in love with Atticus—was practical. Sensible. Fortunately, she knew Atticus knew her, and she was grateful he waited to propose, giving her time to really be comfortable with all their plans.

For four months they dated long distance, and at first it was fine, but after two months, it became incredibly frustrating. She knew at New Year's, when she met Atticus's family, that he was the one she'd want forever, and she'd thought she'd be okay waiting for them to actually be together, but she was wrong. She wasn't happy away from him. By Valentine's Day she didn't want to be in Irvine anymore. By March, she didn't want to be at Novak & Bartley. She just wanted to be wherever Atticus was. Houston. Galveston. Marietta. She just wanted to be with him. She loved him, and now that she loved, she wasn't ever going to stop.

One day during the third week of April he called while she was at work, letting her know that the Bank of Marietta was ready to sell their building, and asked if she'd want to go to Marietta with him and look at the building, and help them decide if this was the right thing, and if he should make an offer. She told him she'd be on the next flight.

"Would you be able to stay for a few extra days?" he asked. "We haven't had much time together lately and I miss you."

"Yes, yes, yes."

"Can you get the time off on short notice?"

"We've survived April fifteenth. I'm sure I can get some time off. But, Atticus, I should tell you, that I've been shifting some work to the other accountants on my team. I've delegating more because I'm ready to move on. This isn't what I want. I want to be in Marietta, in my bookstore. Living there, I could build my client base. I've looked into the accountants there, and most of them are older men, and I think they could use some fresh blood." She hesitated. "I guess what I'm saying is, if you're ready for Marietta, I am, too."

"And if the bank isn't the right place for me?"

"Then I go where you are." She took a quick breath. "If you think that's the best thing for us. If not, I'll just go to Marietta and we'll take it from there."

"I just worry that Marietta is too small for you."

"My world is even smaller here. It's the office, and my condo, and that's it. I have more friends in Marietta than I do in California."

ATTICUS WAS IN Bozeman when she arrived Wednesday at two thirty. He'd already rented a car and had his suitcase in the back. He took her luggage, added it to his in the back of the SUV, and they were off as they had an appointment in Marietta and needed to drive straight to it, if she didn't mind.

She didn't mind.

In Marietta, she expected they would go to the bank. Instead, they went to the courthouse. It wasn't until they were at the courthouse, speaking to the county clerk, that it began to dawn on her what was happening.

"A marriage license," she whispered to Atticus.

"What do you say?" he answered. "Want to get married?"

"You're proposing?"

"Want to get married today? There's no waiting period in Montana."

"Are you serious?"

"Yes."

"Just you and me?"

"Would you hate that?"

"No. I'd love it."

"But of course, if we marry here, we'd have to invite a few friends. The Sheenans and Douglases."

She thought of her father and felt guilty. "My dad should be here, though, and your parents. Especially your parents. I don't think they'd forgive you for getting married without them."

"We could always go to Houston for a honeymoon."

She tried not to wrinkle her nose. "We could," she said slowly, reluctantly.

The clerk returned their IDs and the completed paperwork and wished them well. Atticus took her hand, and held it as they left the clerk's office.

"Well, think about it," he said. "We can always do the wedding here, and a reception there."

She smiled up at him. "Oh, I like that idea. I'm sure your family has tons of friends they'd invite."

"Too many friends," he agreed. "It's not really my thing."

"Or mine." She tugged on his hand on the steps of the courthouse. "I'd love to marry sooner than later."

"What about a big white wedding? Wouldn't you miss all the fanfare and fuss?"

"Oh, no. It's such a waste of money."

He laughed, and kissed her, and then kissed her again, eyes still crinkling with humor. "How did I know you were going to say that?"

"I'm consistent."

"Yes, you are." He hugged her to his side, kissed the top of her head. "But let's head over to the bank, and get this over with so we can plan our future."

They drove a few blocks north to the bank. The sign Bank of Marietta was already gone, and a new historical plaque had been added to the wall, next to the great front doors.

Atticus held a door open for her, and she entered the lobby, and then froze.

It wasn't a bank anymore. It was a restaurant with gorgeous sapphire velvet booths and modern artwork on the walls, the artwork's bright pops of color a vivid contrast to all the white marble.

"You've already bought it," she said, looking around the soaring space that was so beautifully remodeled.

"I did."

"You didn't tell me."

"I didn't want to put pressure on you. I wanted you to make the decisions that were best for you."

"What if I wanted to live in Irvine or Houston?"

"Then I'd manage this from afar, just like my other restaurants." He drew her into his arms, holding her securely. "I want to be where you are. The where doesn't matter."

"I agree." She rose to kiss him. "So, let's get married."

"I think that's a fantastic idea." He kissed her back before shouting into the restaurant. "She said yes."

People poured from the back of the restaurant, familiar faces from Marietta, but also faces from other places… Atticus's parents from Houston, his grandparents and brother from Galveston, Lesley from Queensland, and then there was her father, from California.

Rachel's heart turned over as everyone appeared with glasses of champagne, and a waiter approached with two flutes on a tray.

Atticus handed her a flute, and took the other one for himself.

He faced her and raised his champagne in a toast. "To my future bride, I love you so very much, and I can't wait to make you mine." He glanced at his watch. "Which won't be long as the ceremony begins in less than an hour."

Everyone cheered and drank champagne before Taylor and Sadie stole Rachel away to help her dress for the wedding.

In the end, it was the most magical wedding Rachel could have ever imagined. Atticus had done all the planning, and there were flowers, and tuxedos, flower girls and a ring bearer, and then there was her dress, an elegant white satin dress with delicate cap sleeves, a sweetheart neckline, and a full satin and tulle skirt that made Rachel feel like a princess.

"That was your mother's dress," her father told her, just before he walked her down the red carpet that had been rolled across the marble floor to where Atticus stood with the reverend, waiting for her.

So, she was married in her mother's hometown, wearing her mother's dress, in front of all the people she cared most about.

It was the most perfect wedding, in the most perfect place.

And when the reverend pronounced them husband and wife, Rachel felt so much love, and peace.

She didn't know what the future would bring, but as Lesley had said on Christmas morning, life was short, there were no guarantees, and so Rachel was going to seize happiness, and not let it go.

THE END

Love on Chance Avenue Series

Book 1: *Take Me, Cowboy*
Winner of the RITA® Award for Best Romance Novella

Book 2: *Miracle on Chance Avenue*

Book 3: *Take a Chance on Me*

Book 4: *Not Christmas Without You*

More by Jane Porter

The Taming of the Sheenans

The Sheenans are six powerful wealthy brothers from Marietta, Montana. They are big, tough, rugged men, and as different as the Montana landscape.

Christmas at Copper Mountain
Book 1: Brock Sheenan's story

Tycoon's Kiss
Book 2: Troy Sheenan's story

The Kidnapped Christmas Bride
Book 3: Trey Sheenan's story

Taming of the Bachelor
Book 4: Dillion Sheenan's story

A Christmas Miracle for Daisy
Book 5: Cormac Sheenan's story

The Lost Sheenan's Bride
Book 6: Shane Sheenan's story

ABOUT THE AUTHOR

New York Times and USA Today bestselling author of over fifty five romances and women's fiction titles, **Jane Porter** has been a finalist for the prestigious RITA award five times and won in 2014 for Best Novella with her story, Take Me, Cowboy, from Tule Publishing. Today, Jane has over 12 million copies in print, including her wildly successful, Flirting With Forty, picked by Redbook as its Red Hot Summer Read, and reprinted six times in seven weeks before being made into a Lifetime movie starring Heather Locklear. A mother of three sons, Jane holds an MA in Writing from the University of San Francisco and makes her home in sunny San Clemente, CA with her surfer husband and two dogs.

ABOUT THE AUTHOR

Thank you for reading

Oh, Christmas Night

If you enjoyed this book, you can find more from all our great authors at TulePublishing.com, or from your favorite online retailer.